PUFFIN BOOKS

Bug Muldoon and the Garden of Fear

Paul Shipton grew up in Manchester and went to university in Cambridge. He spent several years teaching English as a foreign language before becoming an editor of school books in English and science. Writing books was not an early ambition of Paul's but he read a lot and dreamed of being the characters in the books he read – a footballer, a space-cadet, a Viking – but as he was no good at football and was always seasick, his ambitions changed and he became a writer instead.

He has recently moved to America with his wife and two daughters where he works as a freelance editor and writer. Although he enjoys life there, he still misses British chips, soap operas, pubs and double-decker buses.

Paul Shipton

Bug Muldoon AND THE GARDEN OF FEAR

PUFFIN BOOKS
IN ASSOCIATION WITH OXFORD UNIVERSITY PRESS

For Vicky, who knows what I'm like when a wasp's around

PUFFIN BOOKS

Published by the Penguin Group
Penguin Books Ltd, 27 Wrights Lane, London W8 5TZ, England
Penguin Books USA Inc., 375 Hudson Street, New York, New York 10014, USA
Penguin Books Australia Ltd, Ringwood, Victoria, Australia
Penguin Books Canada Ltd, 10 Alcorn Avenue, Toronto, Ontario, Canada M4V 3B2
Penguin Books (NZ) Ltd, 182–190 Wairau Road, Auckland 10, New Zealand

Penguin Books Ltd, Registered Offices: Harmondsworth, Middlesex, England

First published by Oxford University Press 1995
Published in Puffin Books 1997
7 9 10 8

The moral right of the author has been asserted

Set in 11/14pt Linotype Palatino and Helvetica
Typeset by Rowland Phototypesetting Ltd,
Bury St Edmunds, Suffolk
Printed in England by Clays Ltd, St Ives plc

1

The sun began to slide over the horizon in disgust. I knew how it felt. It had been a long day, and it wasn't over yet. I felt like I had covered the entire Garden ten times over. I had. My legs were aching – all six of them – and I was getting awful tired of this case. I just wanted to crawl under a rock someplace. Still, an insect's gotta do what an insect's gotta do, especially, when he's being paid.

The name's Muldoon – Bug Muldoon. I'm a sleuth – a private investigator, if you want the full title. I'm the best sleuth in the whole Garden, not to mention the cheapest. Fact is, I'm just about the *only* sleuth for hire in the Garden. The only one still alive, that is.

I was working a missing-insect case. It was nothing special, but in my line of work you take whatever you're offered. It pays the rent.

I had been sitting around in my office that morning, wondering what to do. I had just finished a big case out of town, but now I was back and looking for work. A beetle has to eat, you know? Things were so slow I was even starting to think that I should give the place a spring clean. I was still thinking about it an hour later, when I saw potential clients – three earwigs crawling up by the flower beds. I was curious – you don't see many earwigs down this end of the Garden. They tend to stay up by the garbage cans near the House, the exclusive end of the Garden.

They mooched around nervously by a clump of grass for a while, whispering to each other. Me, I just waited. When they had worked up enough courage, they approached my office, which is a patch of soil underneath a rose bush. They slid their slender brown bodies through the weeds that form my front door. The biggest of the three spoke.

'Mr Muldoon?' he asked.

'Bug. The name is Bug.' (It makes me tense when people call me Mister.) 'What do you guys want?'

The big one introduced himself as Larry. Nice name, I thought. Larry did all the talking. The other two nodded their heads in encouragement.

'It's our brother, Eddie,' said Larry. 'He's gone missing . . .' The other two jiggled their heads.

They needn't have bothered – this sounded like a story I'd heard a zillion times before. A bug going missing isn't exactly big news in the Garden. Still, the three earwigs looked like they expected me to ask some questions, so I did. Anything to oblige a client.

'When did he disappear?' I asked. It seemed like as good a place to start as any.

Larry's antennae waved nervously as he spoke. He was an edgy kinda guy.

'Late last night was the last time we saw him . . .'

'And did he say anything – any indication that he was going somewhere?'

Larry hesitated. It gave one of the other two a chance to chip in.

'He said he was going to the meadow!' he blurted.

Larry shook his head. 'Eddie was always talking about taking off for the meadow some day. That's all it was – talk. It didn't mean anything . . . Eddie was all talk, he'd never really do it –'

I nodded, but I knew better. How many innocent young insects had I met who dreamed of a better life outside of this Garden – in the meadow on the other side of the stream? They thought that life would be easier. They thought they could spend their days there without always worrying about being eaten by a spider, a bird, or just by the bug next door. Now, I like fairy stories as much as the next beetle, but I knew one thing: life was as hard in the meadow as it was in this hellhole of a Garden that we call home. If Eddie had struck out for the meadow, there was no guarantee he had made it. Still, I didn't see any point in turning away clients.

'Could be he headed for the meadow, could be he got stuck along the way. If the second is true, I might be able to find him,' I said.

I told them that I would look for Eddie, or at least try to dig up any information on where he had gone. I told them my daily fee – plus expenses – and they didn't look too worried.

Before they left, Larry leaned forward.

'One thing, Mr – one thing, Bug,' he said. His voice was low so his little brothers could not hear. 'Eddie runs around with a rough crowd. A lot of his friends are wasps. But he's a good kid at heart . . .'

'I'll do what I can, Larry,' I said. 'If I find anything out, where can I contact you?'

Larry looked me straight in the eye. 'We have a little place near the dustbins. We'll be there.'

And then they were off, scurrying into the grass like a trio of amber torpedoes.

2

And so I had spent the whole day tramping all over the Garden – trying to find out what happened to Eddie the earwig.

I started out asking questions around the patio. No one I spoke to could give me much information. I ran into a bunch of young earwigs who told me that Eddie had thought he was a bigshot – always sounding off about leaving the Garden.

Near the trash cans I spoke to a skinny-legged crane-fly who told me that Eddie the earwig was a bug just looking for trouble, and he hoped that he had found it. He wouldn't say any more than that, but suggested that I talk to Eddie's friends, the wasps.

I thanked him politely but decided not to take his advice – in this Garden you don't approach the wasps if you can help it. Not unless you want to be stung to death. Personally, I don't.

I didn't have any leads yet, but I was starting to form a picture of the missing bug. I guessed Larry had been right – brother Eddie had been the kind of insect just itching to get out of the Garden.

I decided to concentrate my efforts on the East Side – the direction the meadow lay in. I questioned whoever I ran into, but no one had spotted Eddie. Worms, beetles, flies – they all came up empty. I was getting fed up. Surely *someone* must have seen him?

I widened my search, heading down further south. Hour after hour I trudged across grass, soil, concrete, and grass again. As the day crept by, I began to think that something strange was going on in the Garden. I couldn't put a feeler on it, but it was somehow different from when I'd left. There was a new tension in the air – the kind of feeling you get when a storm is about to break and you can feel it in your guts – trouble on the way. All the bugs I spoke to seemed edgier, more defensive.

When I told a shield-bug that I was looking for a missing earwig, he answered, 'So what? Tell me who isn't missing nowadays.' Then he scurried off on his business.

That's the way the whole day went. After speaking to dozens of insects, I had made no progress – not a single clue about what had happened to Eddie the earwig. And then I ran into Jake . . .

He spotted me from above and buzzed down to land on a sod of turf in front of me. Jake is a housefly. He's also a sugar addict, owing to the fact that he once landed in a bowl of sugar cubes. Now he couldn't get enough of the stuff. And when he *didn't* get his sugar fix, he began to quiver and shake, which is why some bugs know him as Shaky Jake. Personally, I think nicknames like that are impolite.

'How's it going, Shaky?' I said.

'P-p-pretty good, B-Bug,' managed Shaky Jake. His compound eyes flitted this way and that, and he skittered sideways. I guessed he hadn't had any sugar for a while.

'Still got the sweet tooth?' I asked.

'S-s-still got it.' Then he added, 'Not s-s-seen you for a while, B-Bug?'

'Been away on a case,' I answered. OK – that was the small talk done with. Now down to business.

'Hey, Jake,' I said, 'I need some information.'

'Got a new c-case, Bug?'

I nodded. Jake sometimes supplied me with information, and in return I did him a favour every so often. It was a system that suited us pretty well.

'I'm looking for an earwig, name of Eddie. Young guy – ran with a bad crowd, made a lot of big talk about striking out for the meadow . . .'

Jake thought for a moment. 'I heard an earwig was seen d-down by the compost heap this morning, down by the . . . the . . .'

He couldn't bring himself to say the word. I guess he thought even saying the name might jinx him in some way. I helped out.

'Down by the spider?'

Shaky Jake nodded nervously.

'Did he get away?'

Even as I asked the question, I knew it was stupid: the spider down by the compost heap was enormous. Once you were in his neighbourhood, 'getting away' was no longer a consideration.

So . . . the mystery was solved – Eddie had ended up as a light snack for the spider. Telling Larry and the boys wouldn't be easy. But before I did that, the least I could do was go check out the story for myself. Just to be sure.

I turned to go. 'Thanks for the info, Jake,' I said. 'Go find yourself a piece of candy.'

H-Hey, Bug!' Shaky Jake called after me. 'You be c-careful out there.'

'Don't worry, Jake, I've got no intention of providing the second course.'

Jame shook his head. 'I don't mean with the . . . the *you-know-what*. I mean in general. There's some weird stuff going on in the Garden . . .'

I smiled. 'Things seem the same as usual – lousy,' I replied. But it *was* true that I had noticed a strange atmosphere. And what had that shield-bug said: who *isn't* missing nowadays? What did *that* mean?

Shaky Jake was normally a reliable source of information. He looked around now to check no one was listening, then said, 'W-word is, something's going on with the ants.'

This was news to me. The ants usually kept themselves to themselves. I was interested.

'Something going on, like what?' I asked.

'D-don't know,' said Jake (and I knew him well enough to know that he was telling the truth). 'But it's b-b-big.'

I considered this a moment. 'Thanks for the advice, Jake. Remember to take it yourself.'

And then he was gone. I watched him fly away, until he was nothing more than a black dot racing along the grassline.

I headed south.

The web was huge. It was fixed to an old oil-can on one side and the rake that leant against the compost heap on the other. In a way it was beautiful – the way the fading sunlight caught its strands – but it wasn't quite so beautiful when you remembered what it was for. How many insects had gone to their deaths inside its delicate patterns, I wondered.

I kept a safe distance. The spider sat motionless at the side of the web. It was gigantic. It looked like it should be in the Amazonian rain forest, not at the bottom of some back garden.

And there, suspended in the centre of the web, were the remains of Eddie. Or at least I guessed that's what it was, I couldn't be sure. The body had been wrapped up in the spider's thread, and half of it had been eaten already. It wasn't a pretty sight.

A light breeze blew. The web swayed, but the spider didn't stir. I felt like I should say something.

'So long, Eddie,' I said, though no one was there to hear. Then I turned around and began the long journey up to the dustbins.

When I found Larry and his brothers, night had almost fallen. They were waiting by a crack in the concrete paving stones. I could see they were disappointed I had come alone.

'Any news?' asked one of the two young brothers.

'Sure, kid,' I said. 'I ran into a mosquito who said she saw an earwig this morning over by the fence on the East Side – seemed to fit Eddie's description.'

'What was he doing? Where was he?' chipped in Little Brother Number Two.

'Well, she couldn't remember it too well – mosquitoes aren't too bright, you know? It was something about saying goodbye to his brothers, and letting them know he'd be OK, that he was looking forward to his new life in the meadow.'

The two smaller earwigs looked relieved at this news. They swapped grins. Larry looked less convinced.

'So . . . I guess we owe you a day's pay?' he said warily.

I shook my head. 'Special offer in missing-bug cases today – 100 per cent discount. Let's just say, you owe me a favour . . . OK?'

Larry nodded. I turned and left the three of them to their chatter of what brother Eddie must be doing now. I crawled away and stepped on to the lawn –

it felt good to have grass under my legs again. I don't like concrete.

I didn't know why I had lied to Larry and the boys – it had been a spur-of-the-moment decision. Maybe I'm just a softy underneath this black shell.

But I knew one thing for sure – I needed a drink.

3

It was business as usual at Dixie's Bar. The joint was jumping. It was packed with insects and bugs from all over the Garden, and they were here for just one thing – to have a good time. There were all kinds of species, and no one was eating anyone else. The rule at Dixie's is simple – *If it ain't on the menu, you can't eat it.*

I picked my way through the crowd. A gang of young cockroaches loitered by the bar, on a night out over from the House. A woodlouse was showing off his armour-plating to a moth. She looked bored.

I settled into my usual place and nodded to Dixie. He was lolling at the far end of the bar, nibbling a dandelion stem and talking to a horsefly. He waggled an antenna lazily when he spotted me.

Dixie's a nice guy, but kinda slimy, if you know what I mean. He's a slug. When he came to the Garden a few years back, he set up the bar under the canopy of some rhubarb leaves. I did him a favour one time, and ever since then I always get VIP treatment at Dixie's.

I ordered my usual drink from the ladybird waitress – nectar with a twist of privet leaf – and sat back to watch the floorshow. It was a daddy-long-legs doing a dance routine. The bees in the band were buzzing a pretty wild tune, and the dancer was hot. His six legs moved so quickly it made me tired just watching, so I stopped.

I had come to Dixie's to forget, but I couldn't stop my mind from going over the day's events.

It had seemed a simple enough case: eager young earwig desperate to see the world, hungry spider waiting for an afternoon snack. End of story – and a familiar story at that.

And yet something bothered me about the whole deal. Something was wrong. It tickled at the back of my mind like an itch you just can't scratch. Why had Eddie been down by the compost heap anyway? According to older brother Larry, Eddie always talked of heading for the meadow. But the meadow was in the opposite direction from the compost heap. So what was Eddie doing at the other end of the Garden? Apart from providing dinner, that is. Where had he been going? Why had he failed to notice the spider's web?

What? Where? Why? These thoughts buzzed around my brain like summertime midges. Lots of questions, and no answers. And what about the other stuff – reports of more missing bugs, an atmosphere of tension that permeated the Garden like the smoke from a bonfire? I couldn't shake the feeling that it all had something to do with what Jake had said: trouble with the ants.

I told myself to relax, quit thinking things over. Sometimes stuff happens, and it does no good wondering why.

Suddenly the entrance leaves brushed back and in marched two soldier ants. Gasps of surprise echoed around the bar – you don't see many ants in a place like Dixie's. It's not their kind of establishment.

'Gentlemen, what an honour,' lied Dixie to the two ants as they trooped by. The bar-owner's voice was more slobbery than usual. The ants ignored him. They marched past the first aisle, along the bar and towards the stage. I couldn't see what rank they were. Who can tell with ants? They began to push their way through the customers.

I'm not certain when I realized that they were coming to my table, but sure enough they stopped right in front of me. Great, I thought to myself: the perfect end to a perfect day.

The first one spoke. 'Bug Muldoon,' he said in an emotionless voice. It wasn't a question.

I took a slow sip of my drink and eyed them coolly. 'Who wants to know?'

'You will come with us,' said the second ant. His voice too was flat and lifeless. These were not fun-time guys.

I smiled. 'Relax, boys. Don't be so persist*ant*,' I

quipped. Neither of them got the joke. I wasn't surprised: ants aren't well-known for their sense of humour.

Everyone in the whole joint was straining to hear our conversation. The music had stopped, and the daddy-long-legs was standing still on the stage. He looked confused. Dixie was casting anxious glances in our direction; disturbances like this were bad for business.

'Try again,' said the first ant to his companion. 'I don't think he understands.'

The second ant piped up again. 'You will come with us,' he repeated. 'You will come with us NOW.'

I nodded. I outweighed the two of them put together, but I knew I had no choice. Ants never travel in just pairs. There had to be a whole battalion waiting outside, maybe more. That's the thing about ants – there are lots of them.

I finished up my drink and followed them out. As I walked by Dixie, I gestured towards the tap-dancer on the stage. 'You've got a good act there, Dixie. Look after him.'

'Sure thing, Bug,' said Dixie. 'See you around.' What Dixie was really thinking was that this was the last he would ever see of Bug Muldoon. At least he sounded sad about it.

We stepped out into the cool night air. The moon was riding high – it looked smug and aloof up there, as if it had better things on its mind than what was going on down here. Sometimes I look up at the moon and I wonder what it makes of us, scrabbling around down here in the muck and soil.

I'd been right – a small force of ants waited in battle-formation by the rhubarb leaves that formed the entrance to Dixie's Bar. I guessed there were about forty of them.

The first of the two ants that I'd followed out turned to me. 'We have little time. Follow me.'

He began to march off towards the lawn. I followed, and the whole battalion fell in behind us. What ever was going on, I had no chance of escape, not with so many ants.

'Hey, pal' I called to the ant leading the whole parade. 'You've got the advantage on me.'

He said nothing. I went on, 'You know my name, I don't know yours.'

The ant did not glance at me. 'I am Lieutenant Commander, Third Division, Beta Squadron.'

'That's swell,' I said. 'But what about a name? What do folk call you?'

'I am x437-TKP,' answered the ant. I should have known better – only the upper ranks of the ant colony were given the honour of a name. Everyone else made do with a number.

'Snappy name. Do your buddies call you x4?'

No reply.

'You look more like a "Frank" to me,' I said.

Again no reply. I gave up trying to be friendly.

We reached the edge of the lawn. The grassy terrain was easier going, and we picked up pace. I sensed hundreds of eyes watching from behind blades of grass in the darkness, though I saw no one. Most bugs tend to lie low when there's a column of ants on the march.

They usually have good reason to. Nobody messes with the ants around here. They are the major force in the Garden – more powerful even than the wasps. What they say goes. I'm not saying it's such a bad thing. At least the ants maintain some kind of peace in this rotten Garden.

The Ants' Nest is in the middle of the lawn. People don't know too much about them, and they don't *want* to know too much either. I couldn't help thinking about what Shaky Jake the housefly had said to me: 'You be careful out there . . . there's something going on with the ants . . .'

Suddenly, the ant in front of me – Mr Sparkling Conversation – stopped dead in his tracks. Every single ant in the column behind me stopped that same instant. It was kinda eerie the way they did that all together. Ants communicate with each other with chemical signals they pass along. Means they can react together in an instant. It's almost as if they can read each other's minds.

We were standing outside one of the entrances to the Nest. The hole looked harmless enough, but I knew it led down into a network of tunnels that you could lose yourself in for days. I wasn't keen to try it out.

'I will go first, you will follow,' said x437-TKP.

'Any attempt to escape will be futile.' He began to march down into the entrance that led to the depths of the Ants' Nest.

'No problems, Frank.'

I tried to sound chirpy, but I was starting to get a bad feeling about this . . .

4

I followed the ant I had called 'Frank' down into the tunnel. It was a tight squeeze – I'm bigger than any ant – and I could feel the sides of my shell rub against the soil walls. The rest of the ants followed behind me.

I could see nothing, but whenever we needed to turn, the ant in front would shout out 'Left!' or 'Right!' At first I tried to keep track of the turns, but there were so many that they became a blur in my mind. I knew that we were sticking to the central corridors – there were lots of smaller tunnels which branched off from these, but only an ant could fit through those.

After an eternity of tramping blindly through the tunnels, we emerged into a larger chamber. The lighting was dim, but I could see in here. The only thing was, I wasn't sure I liked what I saw.

Several rows of ants were lined up against the wall. They were clearly a force to be reckoned with – the élite guard of the Ants' Nest. They looked fearsome – they made the squadron that picked me up from Dixie's look as tough as a bunch of greenfly. A few other important-looking ants stood around, but there in the middle of the room was the ant I had been brought to see . . . The Queen of the Nest.

I had heard rumours about her, but – like everyone else I knew – I'd never laid eyes on the Queen. She was huge – seven or eight times bigger than your average ant, with a great bloated abdomen – and she didn't look too mobile. Not surprising, – the last time she'd been outside was years ago, when she'd flown out from the nest she was born in. After that brief flight in the freedom of the great outdoors, she'd landed and founded this colony. Since then all she'd done was stay put, grow bigger, and make little ants. *Lots* of little ants.

My escort prodded me forward and announced, 'Bug Muldoon, ma'am.'

The Queen looked at me coolly. 'So, the infamous Mr Muldoon, private investigator . . . Tell me something – you're a beetle, not a bug. Why are you called Bug?'

'It's a long story, lady. Maybe I'll tell it to you some day . . .'

One of the ants in the Imperial Guard clacked its jaws menacingly at me – I guessed 'lady' was not the correct way to address the Queen.

'Then let me ask you something else, Mr Muldoon,' said Her Majesty. 'How many ants do you think we are, here in our little colony?'

I don't go in much for playing games, but I took a guess to humour the old dame. 'Eight ... ten thousand?' I said.

'Incorrect,' said the Queen. Her voice dropped a notch. 'We are *One*, Mr Muldoon. However many individual ants you may see, the Nest is One – a single, living thing. Every ant lives to serve the Nest. Without it, we are nothing. With it, we are complete.'

I shrugged. 'OK, so I was out by ten thousand. What's the point?'

'The point, Mr Muldoon, is that word has reached me of . . .' She searched for the right phrase. '. . . an unfortunate development here in the Nest.'

She paused for effect. I waited.

'Some of our number have chosen to reject the way of the Nest. They have become . . . *individualists*.' She said this word like it sickened her to utter it.

I cracked a smirk. I had never heard of regular ants showing even a hint of individual personality. It was a well-known fact about them – they just worked for the collective good of the colony. The idea of personal interests – the idea of *self* – was meaningless to them.

But not, apparently, any more. It didn't sound such a bad development to me.

'So what? Is it so bad if a few ants think about themselves for once?' I said. 'Why not let them live a little? Life's too short not to have a little fun . . .'

I could sense a wave of revulsion around the room. I pressed on. 'What's wrong with wanting to be alone and do your own thing for once? You've got to admit – in the Nest you can never be alone. That can't be good for a growing ant.'

'In the Nest you can never be LONELY,' corrected the Queen. 'I don't think you fully understand, Mr Muldoon. Something like this is a threat to be the very foundation of our existence, and IT MUST BE STOPPED . . .' Her voice echoed around the chamber.

'OK,' I said. 'But where do I come into all this?'

'We require your assistance in identifying the perpetrators,' she replied. 'We will, of course, pay you for your services.'

'Hold on,' I said. 'Am I understanding this right? You've got the biggest army in the Garden at your command – thousands and thousands of ants all ready to obey orders to the letter and track these "perpetrators" down . . . but you want a down-at-heel private eye to take the case?'

'Correct, Mr Muldoon. I have vast resources at my command. And yet . . . our troops have been unsuccessful in locating any of the criminals. Is that not so, Commander Krag?'

She cast a fiery glance at one of the bigwig ants sitting near her. I guessed he was the chief of internal affairs, something like that. He had to be pretty high up, having a name and all. The one called Krag nodded his head curtly, and glowered at me.

'The time has come for a new approach,' said the Queen. 'The time has come to employ a freelance such as yourself, Mr Muldoon.'

'And if I don't want the case?'

She turned again to the chief of internal affairs. 'Commander Krag?'

'If he chooses not to co-operate,' said Krag flatly, not even bothering to look at me, 'at least his body will serve a purpose – it will provide adequate nutrition for the larvae.'

'That would be most regrettable,' said the Queen. 'Food is easy to find – abilities such as yours are somewhat rarer.'

What a choice, I thought – either take a case from the Queen of the ant colony, or be eaten alive. It was a tough one, but I went with my instincts. 'OK,' I said. 'I'll take the case.'

Besides, in a funny way I kinda liked the old ant. She was a living legend in the Garden – the grand old matriarch of the Ants' Nest. The Garden had known peace for years now, and that was largely due to the Ant-Queen and the way she ran the Nest. What's more, I was intrigued. Ant individualists? This was something I had to see.

'Very good,' said the Queen. 'Commander Krag will brief you in detail. And, Mr Muldoon? Do not let us down . . .'

I was led away into a side chamber. The ant known as Krag followed me, along with several fearsome-looking soldier ants. Once inside, Krag thrust his little face close up to mine. 'I don't like you, Muldoon,' he snarled.

'Gee,' I said. 'Does that mean the wedding's off?'

'It must be assumed that the Queen knows what she is doing,' Krag continued, 'but I consider it a grave insult to the glorious Ant Army to employ a mere beetle to do our work for us.'

'Hey, pal, I didn't ask for this case, remember? I've just got an aversion to being eaten . . .'

'Silence!' snapped Krag. 'You will do what you can to locate the individualists so that we can remove this cancer from the body of the Nest. As soon as you have any information . . . ANY information . . . you will report back to me. Understood? Even if you discover nothing, you will report back to me in two days' time. Do I make myself clear?'

He leaned closer still, so close I could smell him. 'I have reason to believe that the ringleader of these accursed individualists is an ant with very distinctive markings – a small white patch on her head. It is of the utmost importance that this ant be found. Find this ant, and we might even allow you to live . . . Do you have any questions?'

'Just one,' I said. 'Are you doing anything Saturday night?'

The ant I'd called Frank led me back up to the surface. I tried to get some more information out of him as we went.

'So tell me – what's so bad about a few individualists in the Nest?'

x437-TKP – Frank – paused. If I hadn't known better, I'd have sworn I could detect some emotion in his voice.

'The purpose of an ant's life is to serve the Nest. Each of us is nothing more than a tiny part of the greater whole. An individualist ant makes no more sense than a leg or an eye wishing to live apart from the rest of the body.'

'Don't you ever wish you could think for yourself?' I asked. 'Make decisions of your own?'

The ant shook his head. 'Decisions are unnecessary. There is only one decision – to follow orders and serve the Nest.'

I had to admit, the way he put it, it sounded kinda nice: no need to think for yourself, safe in the knowledge that all the other thousands of ants in the Nest shared the same thoughts as you. It sounded *secure*. Security was something I didn't know too much about.

We had reached the entrance.

'The only thing is – sometimes you've gotta make decisions on your own, whether you like it or not,' I said.

The ant wasn't interested in my words of wisdom – he'd already turned and started back down towards the Oneness of the Nest.

'Nice talkin' to ya, Frankie-boy,' I said.

5

The next morning I started the day with something unusual: I got up bright and early. I didn't like it, but I figured I'd better come up with the goods on this case. (I liked my body, and didn't want it to be eaten. I'm selfish that way.)

Before I'd left the Nest last night, Commander Krag had told me everything his troops had found out – that there were secret meetings of the individualist ants up near the House. He said that his troops had had no luck infiltrating the secret group, or in locating the precise whereabouts of the meetings. The last thing he'd said to me was: 'We will be watching you, Muldoon, we will be watching . . .'

I looked around now to check the coast was clear. The Garden looked peaceful in the pre-dawn light. I wasn't fooled – looks can be deceptive. You have to be careful at this time in the morning: the birds are peckish, and they like nothing better than a nice, juicy bug for breakfast.

I decided the first thing I should do was find

Shaky Jake the housefly. Perhaps he had picked up some information. It was worth a shot, especially as I had no other leads. I set off, just as the sun began to peep wearily over the horizon.

As I pushed my way through the undergrowth I ran into something strange. It was a big lump of gooey pink stuff. I checked it out with my antennae – sugar! It was a piece of bubblegum that some sloppy Human had spat out. I'm not into sugar, but I figured Shaky Jake would appreciate the sugar rush – and it might help to jog his memory – so I picked the piece of gum up and carried on walking with it.

After a few minutes an eager voice cried out from the dandelion patch to my left: 'Hey, Bug!'

I sighed. 'What is it, kid?'

Billy was a caterpillar. He was a good kid, but a little too enthusiastic, if you know what I mean. Especially so early in the morning.

'Watcha got there, Bug?' His voice was so loud it gave me a headache.

'Gum,' I said. 'I'm starting a collection.'

I began to move on, but Billy wasn't done yet.

'Got a new case, Bug?' he shouted. He wiggled his fat green body excitedly.

'Sure thing, kid.'

'Can I come along?' he pleaded, and all the bristly hairs on his chubby body stood to attention.

'Sorry, Billy, I work alone, you know that.'

He couldn't hide his disappointment. 'But how

am I ever going to become a private eye if you won't let me tag along? I've got to learn the ropes, Bug.'

'I stopped. 'Listen, kid, I've told you a thousand times. You're *not* going to become a detective. You've got better things ahead of you, you're not going to be a caterpillar all of your life. One day you'll turn into a butterfly, and you'll be able to leave this stinking, crummy Garden far behind you. See?'

Billy pouted. 'I don't want to be a butterfly! I want to be a private eye like you, Bug!'

I laughed. 'Sorry, kid - nature's got other plans for you.'

I was about to move on, when I became aware of a shadow passing overhead, and a rush of air. The harsh cry gave it away. It was a bird – a magpie – and it had spotted us!

Let me tell you something about bombardier beetles. If anything attacks them, they squirt a jet of stinging chemicals which can scare off anything – a spider, other bugs, even birds. No one messes with a bombardier beetle.

Unfortunately, I am *not* a bombardier beetle. We were in big trouble.

The magpie landed right between me and Billy. It cawed triumphantly, and its beady eyes flitted between the two of us. It couldn't decide who looked tastier.

Billy froze with fear. I had to do something, so I made the bird's decision for it. Still holding on to the gum, I scurried forward. The magpie stabbed at me with its deadly beak. It struck ground. Another couple of centimetres left and it would have speared me.

I changed direction, zigzagged back. The magpie let out a harsh cry of irritation, and plunged its beak down again. Again it missed, but not by so much this time. Its aim was improving.

I made my move. I stopped dead in my tracks and held the bubblegum up high above my shell. The magpie readied itself for the kill. Its towering figure blocked all sunlight. It lunged. At the last moment, I dropped the gum and leapt to the left. The magpie's beak sank straight into the sticky lump.

It reared its head back and tried to cry out, only it couldn't. The gooey lump held its beak firmly shut. The bird waggled its head frantically from side to side to rid itself of the gum, but no luck: the pink lump stayed put. The magpie fixed me with a look of frustrated anger, then flew off for the trees.

'Wow,' gasped Billy, 'that was totally cool!'

'You're too easily impressed, kid,' I said, but Billy was already reliving the encounter. 'Take that, you dirty bird! Eat gum! Nobody eats Bug Muldoon, private eye . . . or his partner Caterpillar Bill . . .'

I shook my head and went on my way.

An hour later I was sitting with Shaky Jake. The sun was already baking hot, and the breeze offered little respite. It was going to be another scorcher.

'I had a present for you – some bubblegum,' I told the fly, 'but I gave it to someone who needed it more than you.'

Jake shrugged sadly and rubbed his front legs together the way that flies do. I suppressed an urge to shudder.

'Doesn't m-matter, Bug,' he said. 'I came across a p-piece of chocolate out on the pavement.' It was true – he wasn't shaking as much as usual. 'What did you w-want to see me about?'

We were underneath the leaves of a rhododendron bush. It was in the shade, but that wasn't why we had chosen it. It made pretty good cover: I didn't want anyone listening in on this conversation. Even then I kept my eyes open.

'What you were saying yesterday – about something going on with the ants. Well, you were right.'

I ran through what had happened the night before. What I told him made Jake live up to his nickname more than ever. I asked him if he'd found out any more. He shook his head.

'N-n-not really,' he said. 'B-but I heard there's someone who's been asking a lot of questions. A new grasshopper working over on the West Side. She m-might know something . . .'

'Grasshopper, huh?' I said. 'Well, right now I'll give just about anyone a go.'

6

I don't usually have much to do with grasshoppers. In my line of work it pays to keep a low profile, and grasshoppers don't know the meaning of the term. They're the Garden's news service. They hear what's going on, and then broadcast it for anyone who cares to listen, and I mean *anyone*. Sometimes they like to change stories around a little – they call it pepping a story up. I call it lying.

But Jake had told me that the new grasshopper in town was different. He said she told it like it was; she knew when to blab and when to keep quiet. That didn't sound like any grasshopper I'd ever met. I decided to see for myself.

It didn't take me long to find the grasshopper. She was sitting in the shade of the picnic table. She wasn't saying anything. I took that as a good sign. Her eyes tracked me as I approached.

'What are you looking at, friend?' Her voice was husky. It sounded like she thought there was something funny going on. Maybe there was.

'The name's Muldoon,' I said. 'Bug Muldoon. I'm a private eye.'

She nodded, but not too enthusiastically. Her slender antennae swayed gently in the breeze. 'I'm Velma. What do you want, Bug Muldoon?'

'A friend of mine told me you might be able to help with a case I'm working on.'

'Depends,' she said calmly.

'On what?'

'On who your friend is, and what your case is.' She was a cool one, all right.

'Friend's a housefly, name of Jake. You know the guy?'

'I heard the name.'

'The case is something big – it's to do with the ants.'

Her tone of amused calm changed like someone had thrown a switch. She sprang forward on those big grasshopper hind legs.

'What about the ants?' she asked urgently. I guess she could sniff a news story.

I smiled. 'Didn't I come here to ask *you* questions?'

Velma's face was close to mine now. I didn't mind. Her voice was an insistent whisper.

'Listen, friend – I may know something, but I don't hand out information for free.'

I liked this grasshopper – she played hardball. My kind of game.

'What do you want?' I asked.

'An exchange of information!' she cried. 'You tell me what you know, I'll do the same.'

I was suspicious. 'Why do you want to find out about the ants?'

'Because I'm a reporter! I'm in the news business, and this is news, buddy. I can smell it! We can work together!'

I thought this over. Usually I work alone. But then everything else about this case so far was unusual – why not this? Not to mention the fact that I was clean out of leads. If Velma didn't provide any clues, I had nowhere else to go.

'Tell you what,' I said at last. 'We'll start off with a little information trade, and we'll see how it goes from there.'

Velma went first. A couple of her news informants had mentioned something odd going on with the ants. They had heard a rumour that there was going to be some kind of secret meeting that day. Velma said she was waiting for the rumour to be confirmed before she did anything.

I looked her in the eye. 'You don't strike me as the kind of grasshopper that waits for anything.'

Velma smiled. 'I do when my sources are somewhat . . . unreliable.'

'Who are your sources?'

'Pair of earthworms. Name of Dax and Dex . . . they hang out over by the vegetable patch.'

When she'd finished, I filled in the gaps. I told

her all about my visit down in the Ants' Nest, and the case the Queen had given me.

'Ant individualists?' gasped Velma. 'I had no idea!'

When I was done, Velma said, 'So what now?' She was still trying to sound tough, but I knew she was shaken.

'I'm going to pay your friends Dax and Dex a visit,' I said.

'Not so fast!' said Velma. 'I'm coming with you. You need me – Dax and Dex aren't the easiest to talk to. I'm used to them. They're a little . . . odd.'

I smiled and thought to myself: who isn't a little odd? But all I said was: 'Lead on, lady.'

Over in the vegetable patch it took a few minutes of Velma calling out before the worms appeared.

At first a pink snout poked out from the black soil. Then the rest of the worm's ribbed body wriggled out into the open. A moment later a second worm emerged from the earth. It was identical to the first.

'Well, well . . .' began the first worm.

'. . . well,' finished the second worm.

'If it isn't . . .'

'. . . our old friend . . .'

'. . . Velma the reporter.'

That's the way they spoke, switching back and forth from one to the other to complete a single sentence between the two of them.

'And . . .'

'. . . who's . . .'

'. . . your . . .'

'. . . friend?'

'Hmmm?'

Velma hopped forward on those long green legs. 'Hi, Dax, Dex. This is Bug Muldoon – he's helping me on a story.'

Two blank faces turned towards me.

'Hel-'

'-lo,' they said.

'Hey, guys', said Velma gently, 'remember what you were telling me about a secret ant meeting? Can you fill in the details? What do you know?'

'What do . . .'

'. . . we know?' asked the worms.

'What *don't* . . .'

'. . . we know?'

'But it's going . . .'

'. . . to cost . . .'

'. . . you . . .'

Velma stayed calm. (I don't know how. Listening to these jokers was driving me crazy.) 'That's OK,' she said. 'Just tell us what you know.'

'It was last . . .' began Dex.

'. . . Tuesday,' said Dax.

'Wednesday!' corrected Dex.

'Tuesday!'

'Wednesday!'

'What do you know anyway?'

The worms squared off against each other.

'A damn sight more than you!'

'Says who?'

'Says me!'

'You and whose army?'

'I don't need any army.'

'If it weren't for me, you'd be bird food by now.'

'Oh yeah?'

'Yeah!'

Their shouting became louder and louder. They ignored us completely.

Velma sighed heavily and said to me, 'It's always like this. They always end up having an argument sooner or later.'

I shrugged. 'Why do they stick together?' The worms were still bellowing at each other.

'They can't leave each other,' said Velma. 'They used to be the same person – one worm – but they got chopped in half by a spade when the Man from the House was gardening. Both halves lived, and they became Dax and Dex. So you see they're really the same person.'

'That's not possible, is it? A worm's only got one head.'

Velma shrugged. 'It may not be possible, but tell that to them. Anyway, they'd never dream of splitting up, but at the same time they drive each other nuts.'

'Sounds like a sick relationship,' I commented.

'It is, but how would you like it if there were two

of you? How well would you get on with yourself?'

I didn't need long to think it over. 'I'd hate myself,' I said.

Suddenly the shouting stopped. The two worms looked at each other for a long moment, and when they spoke again their voices were back to their former gentle whine.

'This . . .'

'. . . is . . .'

'. . . silly . . .'

'. . . isn't . . .'

'. . . it?'

They wriggled and slithered closer together. I looked away. At last the two worms turned their attention back to us.

'So . . . about the ant meeting?' prompted Velma.

They told us.

7

Velma and I made our way towards the House late that afternoon. I maintained a steady pace; Velma hopped alongside. We took the long route so we wouldn't run into anyone who might get suspicious, and we made it to the border of the lawn without incident. We stepped on to the cement.

The rubbish bins were off to the right – a thought popped into my head of Larry the earwig and his brothers – but we headed left, towards the drain near where the meeting was supposed to take place. At one point we ran into a cockroach, who eyed us warily but said nothing as we passed. Roaches can be that way – they don't like other bugs coming near the House.

At last we reached the meeting place. No one was there yet. I looked the venue over: they had chosen it well. This section of the patio was obscured from the Garden by a hydrangea bush. Also deep cracks ran in the paving stones – they were big enough for an ant to pass through, but nothing bigger.

I glanced westwards. Fed up again, the sun had begun its gradual decent. It was time for us to find our hiding place so we could observe the meeting.

'How about in there?' Velma pointed towards the drainpipe. It would have given us a good view if we crawled up inside it, but I shook my head, no. We didn't want to get flushed away by a sudden deluge of water down the pipe.

I knew where we could go. We climbed our way slowly up the brick face of the House, until we reached the lowest window sill. From there we could peer over the edge and see everything that went on below. The ants would never spot us. It was a perfect vantage point.

Now all we had to do was sit and wait.

To pass the time, Velma told me why she'd moved to the Garden: 'Nothing was going on in my last garden. A grasshopper's gotta keep moving if she wants to find the big story.'

'And is this garden any different?' I asked.

Velma fixed me straight in the eye. 'It has distinct possibilities,' she said.

Then it was her turn to question me, and the question she asked was the one everybody gets around to sooner or later:

'Tell me something. Why are you called "Bug" when you're a beetle?'

I shrugged. 'It's a long story. Maybe I'll tell you some day . . .'

While we were getting acquainted, I kept my eyes

on the paving below. The sun glided downwards.

I was starting to think maybe Dex and Dax had been wrong, but then the first ant arrived. It scurried across the paving stones and took up position near the drain. It was followed by another, then another, all coming from different directions. Several ants crawled out from the cracks in the stones. Soon there were about thirty of them down by the drain. They shifted restlessly.

Two of them took up positions away from the others. They were on guard duty. They scanned the patio for intruders, but they never looked up at the brickwork above.

The rest of the ants formed themselves into a circle. One of them spoke. I leaned forward over the window sill and strained to listen.

'Perhaps we can begin,' said the ant in a voice that was quite different from the usual ant monotone. This voice was reedy and emotional.

All the ants began to chant together:

'Self over others.
The One over the Many.
Freedom over rules.
Fun over duty.'

Then the ant who'd started the meeting spoke again. 'In accordance with the rules of the Individualist Club, each individual will introduce themselves by *name* and then share their Uniqueness with us. And . . . *erhum* . . .' He cleared his throat. 'I will begin. My name is Leopold,' he said, 'and I'm going to recite a poem that I've written.'

I exchanged glances with Velma. *Ants writing poetry? Ants named Leopold?*

Leopold began in a sing-song voice:

'I think that I shall never see
a thing as lovely as, well, ME.
My unique personality
Is my happiest discovery.'

I winced. I don't go in much for poetry; I leave that stuff for the bees. From the look on Velma's face it left her cold too.

But the other ants at the meeting were less critical. They murmured appreciation, and waved their antennae supportively.

Another ant spoke up. 'I'm Fran and I'd like to do a jazz-dance which represents the coming of winter.' She began to gyrate slowly, lifting each pair of legs one at a time and waving her body sections to an imaginary beat.

And so on . . . Each ant introduced itself by name – no mention of numbers here – and then went on to do something that expressed its individuality in some way. One of them juggled with tiny bits of wood, which it kept dropping. Another simply jumped up and down and shouted, 'Look at me. Look at me!'

Now, I'm all for individuality, but that doesn't mean I want to sit through an amateur talent show.

I'd found out all I needed – where the individualists met and what they got up to. I was about to suggest to Velma that we'd seen enough, when something stopped me. Another ant was racing across the concrete to join the meeting. She nodded acknowledgement to the two ants on sentry duty, and approached the main group. As she got closer I noticed a distinctive white marking on her head. This was the ant Krag had ordered me to look out for.

The new arrival joined the others, and said in a flustered voice. 'Wait! There's something important I've got to tell you!'

This was apparently a breach of the rules of the meeting, as there was an immediate hubbub of disapproval.

'You know the rules, Clarissa,' said the ant who had introduced himself as Leopold. 'Before we go on to any other business, you've got to share your New Self with us . . .'

'But –'

'Those are the rules.'

'But –'

The others were adamant. 'No exceptions.'

I smiled and whispered to Velma, 'Old habits die hard. What happened to "freedom over rules"?'

Down below, the ant known as Clarissa sighed. It was clear she wouldn't be able to tell them that she wanted until she'd done her turn. She sighed and said that she would sing a song. I groaned inwardly and expected the worst. But what emerged from that tiny ant's body was a sound so beautiful it almost made me weep. Her voice was rich and deep, with a core of melancholy. The song told of lost love, and its mournful refrain hung in the air like summer mist.

I was still listening, entranced by that golden voice, when all hell broke loose. Clarissa stopped in mid-chorus. A nervous mutter ran through the ants.

A low hum in the distance was growing louder and louder.

'What is it?' whispered Velma. 'Bees?'

I shook my head. 'Wasps.'

Immediately the ants began to scurry off in various directions. Several of them disappeared down cracks in the paving, others took off across the concrete. The wasps were not in view yet, but the buzzing was getting louder. We had to move fast.

'Quick!' I said to Velma. 'We've got to follow. You go after Leopold, I'll tail Clarissa.'

And with that we began to crawl down the wall.

8

I hit the ground running and set off after Clarissa. She zigzagged across the concrete, and headed for the lawn. There were no signs of the wasps yet.

Clarissa had no idea she was being followed. Any old bug can follow another, but tailing someone without them seeing you is an art form. Luckily it's an art form that I could give a master class in. On the concrete I hung back, using plantpots and discarded garden tools as cover. Once she got to the grass things were easier: I could maintain a safe distance and keep her in my sights. It was a cinch.

When Clarissa drew close to the shrubbery patch, I made my move. I speeded up, outflanking her on the left, then taking up position right in her path.

When she appeared, I was right in the way. She did not look at me. She just kept her head down and carried on in true ant style. I called out:

'Nice day . . .'

Clarissa didn't stop.

'. . . for a song,' I finished.

Clarissa slowed, then stopped. I seized the moment.

'What's an ant doing all alone out this way?' I asked.

'Foraging duty,' answered Clarissa. Her voice no longer had that rich texture. This was the usual monotone of the ants. I was disappointed.

'And what's your name?' I asked.

Again the lifeless voice: 'I am worker ant, Y-SVR966K.'

I flexed my wing casing thoughtfully then said, 'That's nice . . . but Clarissa suits you better.'

The game was up and she knew it. It was seconds before she spoke again, but when she did her voice was thick with emotion.

'Listen, I don't know what you want, Mr –'

'Bug.'

'I don't know what you want, Bug, but some things are better left alone.'

I shook my head gently. 'Sorry, Clarissa. Not leaving things alone is my job. Perhaps you should just tell me everything there is to know about your little secret society?'

'The Individualist Club?' she asked. 'Is that what this is about? Don't you know about everything else? Don't you–'

She stopped, looked nervously around. At first I wondered what was going on, but then I heard it too. A distant buzzing, still quiet but getting louder and louder. It was the sound of a wasp.

'I've got to go,' Clarissa gasped fearfully. 'I've got to –'

'Can you meet me later?' I asked. 'It's important.'

Clarissa's voice had reached a new high note of fear as the humming of the wasp grew ever closer.

'Yes, yes,' she said (more to get away than anything else). 'I'll meet you in one hour by the statue near the pond . . .'

And then she was gone, pushing her way into the undergrowth. She was just in time too. Moments later a wasp appeared over my head. It hovered menacingly. Its sting looked lethal, and in this case looks *weren't* deceptive. Wasps are the meanest bugs in the garden. I've known wasps that would sting you just for kicks. The bottom line is this: you don't want to tangle with the wasps.

'You! Seen any ants?' the wasp asked me in a harsh drawl.

'Sure – I've seen lots of ants,' I said, 'but not round here and not in the last half hour.'

'What about an ant with a white patch on her head?'

'Nope – but if I see her, you're top of my list to tell.'

The wasp hovered closer, its buzz grew louder. I guess it was trying to intimidate me. I did my best to look unconcerned, and I must have done a good job because the wasp muttered, 'Wise guy,' and flew off to resume its search pattern elsewhere.

Now there's an interesting development, I thought to myself, as the yellow-and-black wasp flew away.

What do the wasps have to do with all this? I guessed I would find out in an hour when I met up with Clarissa.

I filled in the hour thinking the case through. It had been easy enough to find the renegade individualist ants – what had they called it? – The Individualist Club. I had already gathered enough information to go back to the Nest, tell Krag and the Queen what I knew, and pick up my fee. I could probably make it to Dixie's by sundown.

But I couldn't shake the thought that something was wrong. There was more going on than just The Individualist Club. Why had Krag described one ant in particular for me to find? Why had a wasp been so keen to find the same ant? Everyone knew that the wasps and the ants were the two dominant forces in the Garden – they didn't like each other, but there had been an uneasy peace between them for years. So what was going on?

There was a mystery here. One thing was sure: Clarissa, the ant with the golden voice, had some answers.

I arrived early at the meeting point – the pond over on the north-west side of the Garden. At the front of it there's a small statue of a human – I suppose the Man from the House put it there to make the yard look classy.

As far as us bugs are concerned, it makes a good viewing point; you can climb up to the top and see clear across the Garden.

Today, though, I hung around the base and waited for Clarissa to show. The meeting time came and went. Five minutes, ten minutes went by, and still no Clarissa. I was getting restless. Maybe she never intended to come? Maybe she had just been fobbing me off?

But then I heard a noise from behind me. I wheeled round to greet Clarissa, only I didn't see her. I didn't see anything. As I turned, a blow struck me on the head and my world plunged into a darkness as black as a moonless midnight.

When I came to, I was not in the most comfortable situation. For one thing, I was upside down, lying on my back with all six legs waving helplessly in the air. For another thing, I was floating on water. The pond. I had been dumped in the pond and left for dead.

OK, so I was floating helpless and upside down on the pond. I'd been in worse situations, I wasn't worried.

But then I felt a surge of movement as something passed in the water beneath me – something big – and *that*'s when I started to worry.

Let me tell you something about the great diving beetle. They are incredibly strong swimmers, more at home in the water than on dry land.

Unfortunately, I am *not* a great diving beetle. I was in trouble.

9

I usually keep away from the pond – I like water as much as a fly likes tarantulas – but even *I* had heard the stories about the carp. The fish was said to be huge and it ruled the pond like a mean-spirited tyrant. It ate tiddlers, it ate bugs and flies that landed on the surface . . . from what I heard, it was happy to eat anything.

I tilted my head back and looked down into the murky water. I couldn't see anything in its inky blackness. But then something filled the inkiness. It was the carp! It cruised along near the bottom of the pond. Its fat body was mottled gold and white. It looked hungry.

It hadn't seen me yet, but it was only a matter of time. I felt like I might as well have a neon sign on me saying, 'FREE LUNCH– COME AND GET IT!' It wasn't a feeling I liked. Everybody's gotta go sometime, but I never figured I'd end up as fish food.

I tried to flip myself over the right way, so I could

at least try to swim to safety. No luck. My legs just waggled in thin air.

I looked back into the water. Nothing in view again. *Where had it gone? Perhaps it wouldn't see me?* Suddenly the carp swept into view, and it was coming straight for me. Its stupid fish-eyes were fixed on me and its rubbery fish-mouth gaped open ready to start eating. I was a goner – finito. I've never really given much thought to what happens after you die, but as the carp raced towards me, the question flashed through my mind. I braced myself for the end.

But the end didn't come. I felt a weight settle on me from above, and suddenly the carp was further away. I strained my head upwards above the water level to see what was going on. It was Shaky Jake! The housefly had landed on me and he was flying like his life depended on it. It did. His wings buzzed furiously. He was not strong enough to lift me out of the water, but he pushed me along the surface like I was a boat and he was the motor.

I looked back into the pond-water. The carp didn't want to be cheated out of supper. It had speeded up, swishing its tail determinedly. It was close again. I had a nice view of its teeth, which looked good and sharp.

'Quick!' I shouted to Jake. 'Change direction!'

Jake threw us into a sharp right turn. He followed it with a left. I don't know if it was chance or skill, but it was a perfect manoeuvre. He zigzagged across the pond, and made a slalom turn around a lily-pad. He could do no wrong, and I watched with relief as the carp fell further and further behind, until its ugly mug disappeared into the depths of the water. It was a good thing too – Jake was slowing down. He sounded tired.

At last Jake drove us over to the edge of the pond. We bumped straight into it, and the force of the collision knocked me the right way up. I tumbled on to one of the paving stones that encircled the pond. It felt good to be the right way up, and better still to be on dry land.

I looked at Jake. The housefly was panting furiously and shaking like crazy. He looked like he didn't believe what he had just done. Nobody had Shaky Jake pegged for a hero, least of all Jake himself.

'Jake, my friend,' I smiled. 'I owe you a lifetime's supply of pure cane sugar.'

Jake just shivered and shook.

When I'd dried off, Jake and I struck out for the picnic table where I had first met Velma.

Night had fallen. The darkness was still and heavy, and a low blanket of cloud hung in the sky. It obscured all view of the moon. I was glad – I wasn't in the mood for its accusatory one-eyed stare tonight.

I just wondered whether Velma had had any more luck than me that evening.

I needn't have worried. When we got there, at first I thought she was alone. She looked at me levelly, and said, 'I was wondering what happened to you. I figured maybe you were taking your evening nap.'

I smiled, and thought to myself, *everyone's a comedian.*

'Who's your friend?' asked Velma.

'This is Jake – the fly I told you about. He just saved me from becoming a fish's supper.'

Jake grinned and jiggled his head nervously. He was always edgy around new bugs. Velma appraised him coolly, nodded hello, then turned her attention back to me.

'So, you didn't manage to talk with the ant you followed?' she asked.

'I spoke to her all right – just long enough to set up a meeting. She never showed up, and I got a cosh on the head for my troubles. I woke up doing the backstroke in the garden pond.'

Velma's dark eyes danced. I would have joined in, but I didn't know the tune.

'Did you strike out as well?' I said.

'On the contrary,' answered Velma. Her voice was light, and a laugh bubbled beneath the surface like an underground stream. 'I'd like you to meet my new friend . . . Leopold.'

An ant crept slowly out from the shadows behind Velma. It was the ant from the meeting – the one who had recited the poem. He looked jittery, on edge. (OK, I'll say it. He looked *antsy*. Satisfied?) His gaze jumped between the three of us, but settled on none.

'While you were enjoying your evening swim,' purred Velma, 'I was bringing Leopold here back to answer a few questions.'

I shook my head in disbelief. Velma was a hard-nosed reporter, that was for sure. I was impressed.

I drew up to the little ant known as Leopold. 'OK, pal – tell us everything there is to know about your Individualist Club.'

The ant let out a long sigh as if to say 'where to begin?' When he spoke at last, he voice quivered.

'Well, we're harmless really,' he began. 'We meet twice a week and just . . . just be ourselves.'

'Express your individuality?' I prompted. 'Like doing little dances and reading out poems?'

Leopold nodded. 'Artistic creation is the greatest expression of one's individuality.' He sighed. 'We're tired of doing everything for the sake of the Nest. We just want to do something for ourselves for once . . .'

He sounded whiny, but I could see his point.

'I'm only just discovering who I am,' continued the ant. 'Finding out that I have desires and needs of my own. I don't care about the Nest; the Ant-Queen means nothing to me. I'm starting to look after number one . . . me.'

Velma butted in. 'That's not all. Tell him about the spray.'

Leopold made a little huffing noise like it wasn't really an important part of the story. 'A few weeks ago my squadron was foraging for food over by the chrysanthemum bushes. While we were there, the Man from the House came out and sprayed some chemicals on the plants. Some of the spray went on us.'

I didn't get it. 'So what?'

'So . . . a few days later every ant who had been there began to . . . to question the whole idea of the Ant Collective. We started to think about ourselves – our own wants and needs. We started to think of ourselves as individuals. Not long after we formed our club.'

I let out a short, sharp laugh.

'W-what's funny, Bug?' asked Jake.

'Nothing really,' I answered. 'It's just that this whole individualist movement is just a side-effect of some Human's chemical spray. It's an allergic reaction to a weed killer!'

Leopold didn't seem to like my explanation. He preferred to think of the society as 'an assertion of individual rights over group oppression'. I shrugged – whatever he wanted to believe. I had more important things on my mind.

'OK, now I want to know everything else that's going on. You can start with why a squadron of wasps was looking for your friend Clarissa . . .'

'I don't know anything, I –'

'Don't play cute with me, Leo, or you may never

write another poem again.' (I stopped myself from saying that this might not be such a bad thing.) 'What's going on?'

Leopold shook his head. 'I don't know, really I don't.' He paused. 'I do know something was on Clarissa's mind. She hadn't been back to the Nest for a few days, and she was scared about something.'

'But you didn't find out what?'

'The whole point of our society is to allow members the privacy to explore their own personal feelings. I knew something was wrong, but I didn't want to pry . . .' His voice had taken on an edge of desperation. I wasn't convinced.

'Even though you knew she might be in trouble?'

'Yes, I knew, but . . .' Leopold's voice fell to a whisper. 'She did try to talk to me about it a couple of days ago, but I wouldn't listen . . . I . . . I was afraid to get involved. I've got too much to lose now. I was afraid *for me* . . . can you understand that?' He hung his head in shame.

I nodded. One thing I've learned in this Garden is that heroes are few and far between. I didn't blame Leopold for being a coward, even if I did think that his poetry stank. He'd only just discovered himself as an individual – it was a lot to ask him to risk that so soon.

But something was becoming clear. There was something weird going on in the Garden – something bigger than a society of individualist ants.

The wasps had something to do with it, that much seemed certain. But what?

I looked out into the rotten, danger-filled jungle of the Garden. Somewhere out there was the bug with the answer – Clarissa, the ant with the golden voice. The only question was – where was she?

10

The next morning I had to report back to Krag in the Ants' Nest. I left Velma and Jake to look for Clarissa. We told Leopold he'd better lie low. He didn't object.

A sentry met me as soon as I neared an entrance to the Nest.

'Halt,' he said flatly. 'State your name and business.' There was no aggression in the voice, but it was clear he'd let no one pass without authorization.

'Bug Muldoon. Here to see Krag,' I said.

'What is the nature of your visit?'

'Well, I'm not here to catch up on gossip. Just let me through - he'll see me, don't you worry.'

If the sentry was irritated, he didn't show it.

'Follow me,' he intoned, and he turned and disappeared down the tunnel. I followed. It wasn't as dark as my previous visit – gloomy but not pitch-black – and I did better this time keeping track of the labyrinthine twists and turns of the tunnels.

As we continued down, we passed ant after ant, and I found myself gazing into each impassive face and thinking: *What about this one? Is* **she** *a member of the individualists? Or* **that** *one? Is* **he** *one of them?*

We rounded a corner, passing a chamber full of ant larvae. Nurse ants were feeding them grubs and honey. I looked around at the central passageway we'd entered – a broad walk-way with several doors leading off it. If I'd got my bearings right, then the royal chamber of the Ant-Queen was up ahead on the right. The side room where Krag had briefed me would be the third entrance on the left.

'Wait here,' said the guard, and he scurried off to Krag's chamber to announce my presence.

While I waited, an ant walked by. She was carrying a batch of honeydew, the sugary fluid that the ants farmed from aphids in the Garden.

She scurried past the royal chamber, right by me, then veered right into the mouth of a tunnel opposite. She didn't even glance at me.

The guard returned. 'Krag will see you now.'

When I went into the chamber, Krag was barking orders at a row of soldiers. He turned towards me and sneered. 'So, Muldoon . . . what information have you discovered? You will tell me everything you know NOW . . . Have you found the ant with the white markings?'

In my line of work you learn to trust your instincts – sometimes they can save your life – and right now my instincts were telling me one thing: *go carefully*

. . . don't tell him everything, not yet. Something was bothering me. I could feel it in my guts, it just hadn't made its way to my brain yet. I needed time to think things over. Until then, something told me to tell Krag nothing about Clarissa or the meeting I'd witnessed.

What I said was, 'Well, I've got a couple of leads, but nothing positive. I'll need another couple of days –'

'Pathetic!' scoffed Krag. 'I knew it. How could a mere *beetle* succeed where the glorious Ant Army failed?'

I shrugged. 'Maybe the Queen thought I could handle the case with a little more . . . subtlety?' I suggested. 'I've noticed that isn't your strong point.'

Krag shoved his little ant head right up in front of mine. He was shaking with anger.

'Species like you are a disgrace to the insect world,' he spat. 'If it weren't for the Queen's orders, you'd be dead already!'

I smiled. I figured that if I could get Krag mad enough, he might just let something slip. Besides, it was fun, so I decided to jog him along some more.

'And what makes ants so special?' I asked.

Krag's voice rose. 'You know nothing about us, beetle. The Nest is the most powerful force in the Garden, but it has achieved only the slightest fraction of what it might do. We have not yet fulfilled our destiny.'

'Yeah? What destiny is that?'

'Do you know anything of army ants in South America? They do not live cosily in a permanent nest. They are always on the march, camping in temporary settlements, and surging ever onwards in search of food. Every living thing in their path has a simple choice: get out of the way, or die. They are relentless.'

'It sounds like you approve?' I commented.

Krag was about to say something else, but then caught himself, as if he realized he'd said too much already.

'My job is to support my Queen,' he said at last, 'and to serve the good of the Nest. Which means finding these accursed individualists.' He began to turn away. 'Get out of my sight, Muldoon. And the next time you report back, you had better have more information . . . for the sake of your own health.'

I turned and began to follow the guard back up to the surface. As before, it scurried on ahead, without looking back or uttering a word. As I followed, I couldn't shake the feeling that something was wrong.

Suddenly it hit me with the force of a collision with a two-tonne bumble-bee. The ant I'd seen when I was waiting for Krag – she'd been carrying honeydew. It was well known that the Ant-Queen had a fondness for the sweet liquid – so much so that it was banned to all other ants in the colony. So why hadn't the ant taken the honeydew into the royal chamber? *That's* what had been bothering me.

Maybe it was nothing. Perhaps there was simply a room where the ants stockpiled the honeydew for the Queen, but my instincts told me otherwise. My instincts told me something else was going on.

I turned around as quietly as I could, and headed back. It would be a while before the guard noticed that I was no longer following. But I was playing a dangerous game – if any other ants saw me and raised the alarm, I was done for.

The central passageway was deserted when I got there. I breathed a sigh of relief, and pushed my way into the tunnel I'd seen the ant with the honeydew go down. I just about made it, but it was a tight squeeze. If this tunnel got any narrower, I would be stuck. I stepped into the darkness ahead.

Suddenly I heard footsteps approach. I looked around quickly – there was nowhere to run. I began to scrabble at the walls of the passageway. At first they were hard and unyielding, but suddenly I hit a soft patch that gave way easily under my touch. I pushed forward into it, and found myself standing in another tunnel. A secret tunnel that I'd not been able to see!

I raced along this new tunnel, and after a couple of minutes I came to a small cavern where the tunnel forked into two. Which way? I lowered my antennae and ran them over the soil. At last I detected the faintest sickly trace of honeydew. It led off down the tunnel to the right.

I dashed down that one. After a few more twists and turns the tunnel began to widen, and I heard voices from up ahead. I edged forward, and poked my head around the corner.

There were two normal-sized ants inside the chamber beyond – including the one I'd seen earlier – but what caught my attention was the third. It was a queen ant, but not *the* Queen Ant, if you understand what I mean. This one was younger and quite a bit smaller. One of the other ants was grooming this young, wingless queen. The other ant was feeding her the honeydew.

I edged forward a touch more. Bad move – I dislodged some soil. It didn't make much noise, but the sound was deafening to me.

'What's that?' hissed the young queen. She whirled her head round, but I pulled back just in time. I turned around and raced back along the tunnel. I heard her savage cry behind me.

I shoved my way through the tunnel's hidden entrance, and continued to run. I got back to the central passageway, and pelted towards the tunnel that led back up to the Nest entrance.

As I reached the upper levels, I passed several ants coming down the other way. They viewed me with silent suspicion, but none challenged me. On and on I ran.

At last I sensed the glow of daylight up ahead. I had nearly made it.

Suddenly the face of the guard loomed up in front

of me. He must have reached the top, and turned round to find I was no longer following him. So he had rushed down to see what was going on.

'What have you been doing?' he demanded.

I knew I couldn't let him call Krag – the commander was only looking for the slightest excuse to have me done away with. I panted a little harder than I needed to, and said in my dopiest voice, 'Whoo-ee, you're too fast, little fellah! I was shouting for you to slow down, but you mustn't have heard me . . .'

I am not the world's greatest actor, but the sentry bought my amiable-idiot act. All he said was: 'Follow.'

We went back up the tunnel towards the entrance.

It felt good to be outside in the sunlight again – trudging over soil and grass, not lurking down in the underground depths of the Ant's Nest. But questions crowded in on me as I walked. What was going on? Why had there been another queen hidden away in the Nest? A Nest only ever had one queen. Sure, new queens were born every so often, but these would fly away to found their own new nests. But the queen I'd seen had already lost her wings.

And another thing troubled me. What was the connection with the wasps?

There was only one way to find out. It was time for me to have a chat with a wasp . . .

11

You may not think there's much difference between wasps and bees. After all, they're both yellow and black, they both buzz around the garden, they can both sting. Well, let me tell you, there's a big difference. Bees are mostly friendly, in a scatterbrained way. But wasps . . . they're something different. A wasp will sting you soon as look at you. They're mean and dangerous.

There's another difference between the two. Bees are built to drink the nectar in flowers: they guzzle it and then they weave their way contentedly home to the hive, their bellies coated with pollen. Wasps, on the other hand, are designed for eating and chewing. They feed on other insects, fruit – stuff like that. But they do have a fondness for nectar as well. They view it as a special treat, and I was relying on this fact when I decided to have my little chat with a wasp.

I selected a flower, set up my trap and waited.

And waited . . .

In my line of work you get used to waiting. It comes with the territory. I spent the time watching the Man from the House, who was out in the Garden pushing the device known as a lawnmower across the grass. As I looked at him, my mind was flooded with familiar questions – *What goes on in that big mammalian brain? Is it* anything *like the way we insects think? Who are you, human? What do you think about, what do you hold dear? Do you ever see me and wonder what goes on in the mind of Bug Muldoon*?

No answers presented themselves. I went on waiting.

It was a long time before a wasp appeared. I heard its buzz first – a low angry sound that I could just make out over the whirr of the Human's lawnmower. That wasp's buzz was the sound of trouble, except if there was any trouble today I was planning on being the one to dish it out.

The buzzing stopped. I peeked out from under my leaf cover, careful not to let my head show. The wasp had landed on a flower a few feet away. It began working its way inside the flower to get at the nectar within. I heard its greedy slurp.

After a few seconds the wasp was in the air again. Its buzzing filled my ears. *Come on,* I willed it, *come to this flower – lots of nice nectar here – come to this one.*

My luck was in. The wasp hovered a moment longer, then its hum grew louder as it flew towards the flower right above me – the flower I had specially prepared. I looked up and saw its yellow-and-black body through the petals above. I waited until it was right within the flower, then I tugged hard on the vine I had threaded through the flower. The petals pulled shut around the wasp.

It was stuck.

I secured the trap and gave the wasp a few minutes to realize the predicament it was in. Its buzzing grew angrier and angrier as it tried to escape. I found the noise strangely relaxing.

At last I climbed up the stalk and spoke to where its head was.

'Comfortable enough in there?' I asked. I'm friendly that way.

'Who is this?' rasped the wasp. 'How dare you! Let me out!' He said some other stuff as well, but I don't think I should repeat language like that here.

When he was done, I asked, 'What do you know about a secret organization of ants?'

The wasp's answer was again unrepeatable.

I smiled. 'I hope you don't talk that way back home in the Wasps' Nest,' I said. 'OK, try this one – why was a squadron of wasps searching for an ant by the name of Clarissa? An ant with a white mark on her head?'

The same reply.

I wasn't getting far. I decided to let him cool off for a while, so I took a walk. A nice long walk. Maybe he'd be more talkative after that.

I wandered back to my office to check if Velma

or Jake had left any messages in the soil. They hadn't. But as I was walking away from my office, I couldn't shake the feeling that something was different. Suddenly it clicked: normally I can't leave the office without Billy the caterpillar pestering me. But today there was no eager cry of 'Hey, Bug!' There was no sound at all.

I looked around anxiously, hoping the magpie hadn't returned to finish the breakfast I had so rudely interrupted the day before.

Then I saw it. Billy was not dead, but he *was* gone for ever. His life as a caterpillar was over.

He hung upside down from the stem of a plant over in the nettle patch. He was dead to the world, for he had entered the chrysalis phase. He would stay that way for a few weeks while his body reconstructed itself. When it was over, he would emerge into the sunshine as an entirely new creature, a butterfly. Just imagine – you go to sleep a caterpillar and you wake up as a butterfly! How can a creature be two such different things within one lifetime? Beats me.

Of course, after metamorphosis an insect remembers nothing of its former life. Me, I have no memories of when I was a larva. And Billy would remember nothing of his life as a caterpillar, nothing of his wild ambitions to be a private detective. He would remember nothing of me.

I took a last look at Billy, and I was filled with a terrible unease. This stinking Garden was already dangerous enough for little guys like Billy. And now things were getting worse – this case I was working on was big. Something bad was going on in the Garden – something that made it even more dangerous for the little guys – and it was bigger than just a harmless group of ant individualists.

I knew it was my job to find out what was going on. It was time to get some answers. It was time to renew my questioning of the wasp.

When I got back to the flower-trap, a couple of hours had passed and the wasp was feeling a bit more talkative. It's funny how being trapped without food can have that effect on you.

I put on my best tough guy voice. 'OK, we'll try again. Why were you after the ant named Clarissa?'

'Ants don't have names,' snarled the wasp contemptuously from inside the trap.

'That's true,' I agreed, 'but then wasps don't get caught in flower-traps either, and yet look at you, buddy-boy.'

He didn't have an answer for that. I asked again about Clarissa, and to jog his memory this time I gave him a jab in the side.

After the twentieth time of asking, he gave in. 'We were looking for her because she was snooping where she didn't belong, and she heard something she shouldn't have heard. She knew about the Plan . . .'

I didn't like the sound of this. 'What plan is that?'

There was a long silence. When he spoke again

it was with such arrogance you would have thought that *he* was the interrogator and *I* was the prisoner. This is what the wasp said:

'The Plan that's going to sweep dirty beetles like you clean out of the Garden. That's what you are, isn't it? A dirty beetle. Well, your days are numbered, pal. The new alliance between wasps and ants will destroy everything that gets in its way. The Garden is on the threshold of a new era . . .'

It was a cute speech, but I couldn't help butting in. 'The Ant-Queen'll never go along with that.' Everyone knew that the Queen had little time for the wasps. I couldn't believe that she would form an alliance with them. The wasp had to be bluffing.

But what it said next sent shivers through my exoskeleton. 'Maybe the Ant-Queen's days are numbered,' he gloated.

I was about to demand what he meant, but right then my luck ran out. A squadron of wasps buzzed into view. There were five of them, flying low across the grass in an attack formation, and they had spotted me. They didn't look like they wanted a friendly chat, and they were coming this way . . .

I was back in that familiar place – deep, deep trouble.

12

Like most beetles I can fly, but I'm not very good. I can't compare with the great insect aviators like flies and bees, so I prefer to keep all six legs on the ground. However, I knew I had got no chance of escaping the squadron of wasps on foot.

I scuttled forward, opened my wings and took to the air. The five wasps fell into a new formation for pursuit. I zigzagged right and left, flying low over the lawn. That didn't shake them off at all. In fact, they were gaining on me.

I started climbing high, riding the warm air currents of the summer sunshine, then swooping low again. Still no luck: the wasps were more accomplished flyers than me by far. They weren't even straining, while I was flapping my wings with more and more desperation. And all the while I could hear the ominous buzz behind me, getting closer second by second.

I banked left, and flew into the shade of the apple tree. I thought maybe I could lose them in there. I looped and circled the leaves and branches, zipping in and out. When I thought I was out of sight I plummeted down to the ground. Maybe I could hide out for a while? Several apples had fallen from the tree. One of them had gone beyond ripe – it was rotten. *Perfect*.

I rushed up to it and pushed my way through the puckered brown skin of the fruit. I figured it would be a good place to hide out (even if it didn't smell too good). I worked my way right inside the squishy flesh of the apple, and listened to the wasps circling above. They sounded puzzled, they didn't know where I had gone. That suited me just fine. I let out a sigh of relief.

I shouldn't have. Something within the clammy darkness of the apple pushed its little head right up to mine, and shouted, 'OY! This is my apple! Clear off and find your own!'

It was a maggot. It must have been happily munching its way through the apple, when I had so rudely shown up.

'Listen,' I whispered. 'I just want to hang out for a couple of minutes. I won't eat anything. I don't even like apples.'

'Well, that may be so,' bellowed the maggot, 'but you can just find another apple to hang out in, can't you, buster!'

For a little maggot his voice was impressively loud. I heard the wasps' buzz get nearer.

'Keep it down, buddy,' I hissed.

'Oh, keep it down,' is it?' roared the maggot. 'Well, let me tell you something, Mr-Keep-it-down. This is my apple, and I shall be as loud as I like.' Then he began to shout in a deafening sing-song, 'LA, LA, LA . . . LA, LA, LA . . . loud enough for you? . . . LA, LA, LA . . .'

I was about to reach out and shut the little twerp up – nothing permanent, you understand – but before I got to him he wriggled up and stuck his head out through the top of the apple skin. 'LA, LA, LA,' he continued to shout, 'INTRUDER IN THE APPLE! LA, LA, LA!'

I heard one of the wasps cry out, 'Down there!'

Damn! I backed up out of the apple, shook the apple gunk from my body, then glanced upwards. The wasps were hurtling down towards me in a blur of black and yellow.

I unsheathed my wings and took to the air once more. I was getting tired. My body is too heavy for my little wings, and they were feeling the strain by now. But I couldn't slow down – not when the wasps were so close.

I was approaching the pond now – the home of the big old carp that had tried to turn me into supper yesterday. As I flew over the water, I could see the massive golden bulk of the fish below. The beginnings of a plan seeped into my brain.

It was time to do something about these wasps.

I flew low over the surface of the pond and slowed my speed right down. One of the wasps detached himself from the squadron and went into a dive. His plan, I suppose, was to swoop down from above, grab me in mid-air and carry me off.

I continued flying as slowly as possible, like I was on an afternoon joy-flight – the wasp continued to plummet, it was almost upon me, two seconds, one second . . . at the last moment I swerved sideways. I felt the wasp brush past me, as it shot downwards like a bullet, straight into the waters below. The last thing I heard was a surprised 'ERK?' before it disappeared into the water. PLOP!

I didn't stick around to see if the carp managed to get the wasp. I flew off at top speed again. *One down, four to go.* But I knew they wouldn't fall for such a simple trick a second time. What could I do now?

Then it struck me. The Man from the House was still plodding up and down the grass, pushing his lawnmower. I knew what I had to do. It was crazy, but it was my only chance.

I turned right and flew flat-out for the Man. The wasps were so close to me now they could almost reach out and grab my back legs. Almost, but not quite. The air was filled with the din of their furious buzzing, and my head was filled with the thought of their deadly stings.

I altered my flight path so that I was on a head-on collision course with the Man. Suddenly, I swooped low, straight for the mower itself. The wasps followed, hot on my tail. The metal casing of the lawnmower loomed in front of me, it filled my field of vision. I raced through the spray of cut grass, and straight on – straight towards the whirring blades of the lawnmower.

I shot through a gap between two of the blades, adjusted my angle of elevation a touch, then shot out through a second gap between the blades at the back of the mower. It was an act of precision flying.

As I soared up into the air once more, I couldn't help sneaking a look behind me. All four wasps had followed me into the path of the lawnmower. Only two emerged on the other side. The other two had not been skilful or lucky enough to avoid getting mangled by the blades.

That was three down, but there were still two to go and I was close to exhaustion. I couldn't fly much further, and the two wasps behind me sounded fresher and angrier than ever.

I was slowing down. I urged myself to push on, to fly faster, but it was no good. The inevitable happened. Two pairs of legs grabbed hold of me – one on either side. The game was up – escape was impossible. The wasps had me.

I stopped flapping, and told myself to enjoy the ride as they carried me off towards their nest. A single thought pounded through my brains: *there has to be a better way of earning a living than this . . .*

13

The Garden falls into two main sections. The half near the House is well-maintained by the Man – the lawn, the pond, the bird bath, the apple tree, and the flower beds – all neat and tidy. But at the back of the Garden lies wilder country. A tangle of bushes and weeds runs free here. The Man in the House never bothers with it, except to cut back the parts by the footpath so he can get to the shed. Next to the shed is the compost heap, the domain of the giant spider. A wooden fence marks the far barrier of the Garden. It runs in a straight line, apart from where the tree on the other side has forced it to bulge out.

The wasps have their nest in the roots beneath this tree. And it was there that the two wasps carried me now. They landed at the foot of the tree, and forced me down into the entrance of their underground nest.

As they shoved me into the opening, one of the wasps snarled, 'So, you're the one who has been causing us so many problems.'

'Anything to oblige,' I answered.

'We thought your dip in the pond might make you less enthusiastic,' said the other. 'Unfortunately, it didn't – unfortunately for you, that is.'

So it had been the wasps who had ambushed me when I was waiting for Clarissa, then left me for dead belly-up in the pond.

'I'm not so easily discouraged,' I said.

I was pushed down into the nest. We made our way past row after row of hexagonal cells. Some of them were packed with food. Others were used for a different purpose – they contained eggs laid by the Wasp-Queen. I looked at those eggs and considered how small and innocent they looked – it was hard to imagine that one day they would be wasps.

As we went further and further down, I felt the hostile stare of hundreds of wasp eyes upon me. Wasps' nests are like ants' nests in some ways: everyone has a job to do – some wasps tend the Queen, others nurse the young, others get rid of waste, and still others fly out in search of food. But in other ways, a wasps' nest is very different: unlike ants, the wasps are given to fits of temper, even among themselves. There isn't the same feeling of the Nest as a single thing. The Wasps' Nest felt like a fight waiting to happen.

'Where are we going?' I asked one of the two wasps who prodded me along.

'You're going to meet your maker,' he answered. 'But first you're going to the royal chamber. The

Wasp-Queen wants to see you before you die.'

I said nothing, but my mind was racing. If I was being taken to see the Queen, I was at least in with a chance. My only hope lay in persuading the Wasp-Queen that I had not been interfering with wasp business.

There was just one problem: rumour had it that the Wasp-Queen was crazier than a barrelful of bed bugs. Whereas the Ant-Queen was dependable, the Wasp-Queen was notorious for her wild mood swings. One moment she might be giggling and chatting. The next moment she could be ordering her guards to sting you to death. It was said that Death was never far away when you were in the presence of the Wasp-Queen.

We came to the entrance of the royal chamber, and I was hurled inside. The room was a sea of yellow and black – it was filled with wasps, but it was dominated by the presence of the Wasp-Queen.

A quick glance at her wild eyes told me everything I needed to know – she lived far out in the land known as 'Crazy'.

'Who is this rugged young fellow?' burbled the Wasp-Queen.

'The beetle,' answered one of her aides. 'The one who's been poking around.'

The Wasp-Queen's eyes danced like speeding fireflies.

'Naughty, naughty, naughty beetle,' she said merrily. I smiled as nicely as I could under the circumstances, and listened to the terrible buzzing sound within the Wasps' Nest. I guessed it was nothing compared to the buzzing that went on within the Queen's fevered brain.

'And what is your name, O naughty beetle?' sang the Wasp-Queen.

'Bug Muldoon, ma'am.' (I figured it wasn't the time for smart answers.)

'And why are you called BUG, Mr buggy buggy bug-bug?'

'It's a long story, your majesty. Perhaps I'll tell you one day . . .'

Bad answer – the Queen's sunny expression changed like a cloud suddenly blocking the sun. It scrunched up into a nasty pout.

'You will tell me *now*, or you will die!' she shrieked.

I stayed calm. 'The thing is, your majesty – it's kind of personal.' I gestured at all the wasps that crowded around us. 'I'm too shy. Now if just you and I were together, that would be different . . .'

This answer seemed to please the Wasp-Queen. She giggled long and hard, a high and hysterical sound that was far beyond the realms of normal laughter.

When the crazed giggle subsided, one of the Queen's aides leaned forward and whispered, 'He knows about the Plan, your majesty. He must be . . . disposed of.'

'But I like him,' sighed the Queen huffily. 'I like

you, Bug Muldoon. I'm sorry I'm going to have you killed.'

'Hold on,' I said. 'What if I promise not to tell anyone? Then you could just let me go, couldn't you?' (It was all I could think of at the time.) To my amazement, she went for it.

'Really?' enquired the Queen. 'Your most solemn promise?'

I tried to remember all the promises I had heard young larvae saying. The best I could do was:

'If I should break my insect word,
May I get eaten by a bird,
And if this promise be a lie,
Let your wasps sting me till I die.'

'Bravo!' gurgled the Wasp-Queen. 'Well said! That seems good enough for me . . .'

I couldn't believe my luck. It was beginning to look like I might just live to see another day after all.

But then I heard a familiar voice from across the chamber. 'I'm afraid the word of a *beetle* cannot be trusted, your majesty.' I knew that voice, and my heart sank as I heard it.

It was Krag! The ant commander was accompanied by two of his élite guard. I wheeled round to face him. He looked tiny surrounded by wasps, but he walked with the same arrogant swagger.

'So, you're the ant traitor,' I said. 'I might have known.'

'I am no traitor,' spat Krag. 'Everything I have done is for the greater good of the Nest. And if that greater good means that the Ant-Queen must be removed, then so be it. The days of peace are over! The days of ants farming aphids and foraging for scraps are over! A new golden age is about to dawn. When the old Queen is overthrown, the great ant-wasp alliance will march forth and conquer all in its path. Those who do not yield will be destroyed . . .'

'Just like the army ants of South America?' I asked. 'You're crazy.'

Krag just turned to the Wasp-Queen.

'Do not be fooled by this beetle's smooth words, majesty. He is an enemy of the Alliance, and must be destroyed.'

'Oh, very well, Kraggy-waggy,' answered the Wasp-Queen coyly.

'Wait!' I shouted. 'I can still be useful! I can find Clarissa for you.'

Krag shook his head and smiled a smile that held no sympathy. 'If only you had done that sooner, everything might be OK for you. We might even have let you live. But you had to keep on poking around into everything else, didn't you?'

'I can still find her!' I said. 'I've spoken to her once already. I would've found out more except that your wasp friends decided to give me a swimming lesson.'

'Yes,' said Krag. 'A simple misunderstanding. They were not aware that you were acting on my instructions. But as for your further services, I regret to say that they are unnecessary. Time has run out for you.'

A couple of wasps entered the room. Wedged between them was the ant known as Clarissa. She looked small and vulnerable in between those yellow-and-black brutes. Her eyes surveyed the royal chamber nervously.

'We found her hiding out near the fence,' reported one of the wasps.

'Splendid!' declared the Wasp-Queen. 'Then I suppose it's time!'

'Time for what?' I asked, although I sensed I would not like the answer.

'Time for you both to die,' she answered chirpily. 'Guards – take them to the spider!'

14

Two burly wasps grabbed hold of me and marched me out of the nest. When they reached the entrance, they took to the air, carrying me between them. I saw that another wasp was flying alongside us, carrying Clarissa.

The flight didn't take long. We banked right and swooped low over the compost heap, then suddenly they let go of me. There was no time to unfurl my wings, I dropped like a stone.

Something soft broke my fall – something soft and deadly. It was the web of the giant spider, and I was caught fast in it. A moment later Clarissa landed next to me. The whole web shook. Clarissa let out a cry of horror as she realized where we were. She struggled frantically to get out.

'No use,' I said. 'No way out of a web like this – not unless you have help.'

At last she stopped struggling. We were both trapped, and it was just a matter of time before the spider returned. Clarissa turned her head to look me over.

'Who . . . who did you say you were again?' she asked.

'The name's Bug Muldoon,' I answered. 'I'm a detective. I'd say it's a pleasure to meet you again, but under the circumstances . . .'

'And what have *you* got to do with all this?'

'Hold on,' I said. 'That's my question – what have you got to do with all of this?'

Clarissa blinked rapidly. She did not speak, but I could tell the words were building up inside her. At last they poured out.

'It's been horrible!' cried the ant. 'I was just a normal ant until a couple of weeks ago. Saving the Nest was everything to me. But then I started to have other feelings – new feelings – like the Nest wasn't enough. And there were others who felt the same, we –'

'I know all about the individualist society,' I interrupted. 'Tell me about Krag.'

And so Clarissa told me what had happened.

'I was going to a society meeting. I was taking the long way so no one would spot me, and I was far from normal ant routes. But as I crawled along the side of the garage, I saw something weird. I crept closer for a better look, using a clump of weeds as cover. It was Commander Krag, and he was talking to some wasps. They were laughing and talking about the "New Order" once the Ant-Queen was assassinated. That's the word they used – "assassinated". I couldn't believe it! Krag was asking them if the Wasp-Queen could be trusted – she had a reputation for being unpredictable – but the wasps just laughed and said they could guide her to do what they wanted.

'I tried to creep away, but my movement caught their attention. Krag looked around, and our eyes met. Someone shouted "Get her!", and the wasps began to fly towards me. I was near a crack in the concrete, so I scurried down it and got away. I didn't know what to do. I couldn't tell the ant authorities – I had been breaking the law myself by going to the Individualist meeting. I tried to tell someone in the society –'

'Leopold?' I asked.

'Yes! But he said the whole point of our society was to be individuals, so I should look after my problem *as* an individual. I think he was scared.'

'I think you're right,' I said.

'Anyway, I stayed away from the Nest for a few days. In the meantime, word got back to the Ant-Queen about our society. She was furious. When Krag heard about it he realized that I must be a member of the individualists, and that I had been on my way to a meeting when I saw him. He volunteered to locate the society. What he really wanted to do was locate – and silence – me.

'He set all his troops on the job, but they had no luck. The Queen was unhappy with their lack of progress, and she decided that a freelancer might have better luck. That's where you came in. Of course, the Queen knew nothing about Krag's plan.

'Krag wasn't happy about you getting the case, but he figured that if you found me, then you'd save him a job. And if you found out too much about his Plan with the wasps, he could easily have you killed.'

I nodded. 'It's a pity he forgot to tell his wasp friends I was on the case – they nearly killed me anyway, over at the pond.'

'They just thought you were meddling,' said Clarissa, confirming what Krag had told me back in the wasp's rest. She went on: 'Anyway, since then I've spent my time alone, hiding and surviving as best I could. It's been . . . lonely. It's hard for an ant to be alone, even an individualist ant.'

I remembered what the Ant-Queen had said: what was the line between loneliness and being alone? It beat me.

'One more question,' I said. 'When is the assassination going to happen? When does the Ant-Queen die?'

'At midday on the day before the next full moon. When's that?' she asked.

I sighed. 'Today.' I glanced upwards. Judging from where the sun was it would be midday very soon.

So that was the story, I thought to myself. The individualist society was unimportant. Krag had wanted to find Clarissa only so he could protect his treacherous plot to kill the Queen. The young Queen I'd seen in the Nest must have been the replacement he would put on the throne. A new Queen that would do whatever Krag said. And then the armies of the ants and the wasps would march and fly forth together, intent on destroying all in their path. The Garden was doomed, and I was powerless to prevent it. I was spider-food.

I was snapped out of these thoughts by a sudden movement. Something thin and brown began to emerge from an empty tin can that lay several feet away. Was it the spider's leg? Clarissa and I watched with dread.

But what emerged was not the spider. It was an earwig, and though I'd never seen him before, I recognized him from the description I'd been given.

'Hi, Eddie,' I said.

15

Eddie the earwig was stunned. He edged further out of the can.

'How . . . how do you know my name?' he asked.

'I'm a detective. Your brothers hired me to find you. I was sloppy. I figured you'd ended up as spider food.'

At the mention of the word 'spider', Eddie shuddered in revulsion.

'What did you tell my brothers?' he asked.

'That you'd gone to find your fortune in the meadow.'

'That's nice,' said Eddie. 'I bet they liked that.'

'Sure they did. So how about helping us get out of this web, Eddie?'

The earwig's head jerked violently from side to side. He was clearly an insect on the edge. He refused to meet my gaze.

'Can't,' he said. 'Can't interfere. That's the rule. I don't – can't – look at what goes on out in that web . . . all the bugs that get eaten . . .'

I saw my opportunity.

'Yeah, but you can't help hearing it, can you?'

Eddie nodded. 'It's the screams that get to me! I can't stand the screams. First the bugs beg for mercy. The spider just laughs at that. Then the eating begins – the horrible sucking and slurping sounds, and then the screams . . . it's eaten dozens and dozens since I arrived.'

He looked up at me with a dreadful, hunted look. 'It doesn't just eat to live – it gets a kick out of it.'

'So what are you doing here?' I asked.

Eddie's voice was soft, full of regret. 'I used to think I was a bigshot. I hung around with a gang of wasps, doing odd jobs for them. Then one day they told me there was a bigger job for me. They said something was going on between the wasps and the ants . . . a Plan. I didn't ask the details. All I had to do was keep my ears open and tell them if I heard any bugs getting suspicious about the Plan.'

'And what happened to bugs who got suspicious?'

'They disappeared. The wasps told me they'd been taken to another garden. I didn't know about this place, I –'

'So what went wrong?' (I wanted to hurry him along. I wasn't too happy stuck up on that web.)

'Some bugs on the patio began to get suspicious of me,' said Eddie, 'and how I was always around when the wasps took someone away. The wasps said I couldn't put the Plan at risk, so they brought me here and told me to lie low until I got further instructions. They said the spider wouldn't touch me 'cause it would have enough food coming to it. They were right. The wasps fly bugs in, and the spider does the rest.'

So . . . the wasps were using the spider to get rid of anyone who suspected their glorious Plan. I had to admit, it was a neat system.

Clarissa spoke up. 'You have to help us,' she cried.

'I . . . I can't,' said Eddie desperately. 'The wasps said they'd look after me in the New Order.' He sounded like he no longer truly believed what he was saying. 'I've just got to lie low.'

I took a guess. 'And do you really think the spider's going to be happy to remain just a hired killer? Don't you think he's going to want more than that?'

Eddie could hardly speak for the shakes. 'I . . . I've heard the spider saying something about cutting a new deal. Being joint ruler with the wasps and the ants. What does it matter? I'll just lie low . . .'

I knew a spider like that wouldn't stop at being joint ruler of the Garden. It would let the ants and the wasps do the hard work, then it would take over.

'Just lie low . . .' Eddie was burbling.

'And listen to more bugs being eaten?' I demanded. Then I said the magic words: 'Tell me something, Eddie – what if the next one up here is your brother Larry? What will you do then, huh?'

The question hung in the air like a thundercloud. Eddie was in an agony of doubt. 'Even if I wanted to help,' he said, 'I couldn't. I'd just get stuck in the web myself.'

'Not if you use that bit of glass,' I said. I nodded to where several shards of broken glass lay on the ground. Eddie stared at them, but he did not move.

'PLEASE,' implored Clarissa, and her voice rang with sorrow and desperation. Even I was moved.

Eddie must have been, as well. He moved slowly out of his tin can and picked up a shard of glass, then approached the web.

'I must be crazy,' he muttered to himself, though his eyes said that this was the first sane thing he had done in a long while. He leaned forward and began to slice carefully through the gooey strands of web that bound Clarissa. It was a tricky job, but after a couple of minutes, the ant was free.

Eddie turned towards me. He began to cut the first strand, and he said something, but I didn't hear what. I was too busy staring at what had just appeared on the far side of the compost heap. The spider! It looked even bigger than before. It looked like death on eight legs, and, though it had not yet seen us, it was coming this way.

'Hurry,' I hissed. Two of my legs were free now, four still stuck.

Eddie sensed my fear. He looked around, and froze.

'Cut!' I yelled. Eddie began to move again, sawing at the strands, all the while babbling, 'Oh no, oh no, oh no . . .'

The spider had seen us. It broke into a run. Its spindly legs were a blur.

'Faster!' I shouted.

'Oh no, oh no, oh no . . .'

Four legs free now, two to go – Clarissa was scurrying away as fast as her six legs could carry her – the spider had rounded the top of the heap, and was charging downhill – 'Oh no, oh no, oh no,' wailed Eddie, but he didn't abandon me.

The glass flashed and another leg was free – the spider was close enough for me to see its eyes – I willed Eddie to hurry up on the final strand, but he dropped the shard of glass!

The spider was close enough for me to see its hungry jaws, close enough to see the hairs on its legs! Eddie picked up the glass – the spider was on the home straight – the final piece of web broke with a SNAP! and I flopped forward, I was free – the spider was almost upon us – I raced forward – the spider fell upon Eddie, who had cast aside the splinter of glass.

'Go!' shouted Eddie the earwig from the grips of the spider's jaw. And then he uttered his final words: 'Tell my brothers . . . I'm sorry.'

I ran to catch up with Clarissa. I didn't look back and I tried not to listen as the spider began to eat.

16

The sun was already nearing its zenith in the sky. We didn't have much time. We stopped just once, hiding behind a clump of weeds as a squadron of wasps flew overhead in a V-formation. They were on their way back to their nest.

After that Clarissa and I moved fast, and in ten minutes we arrived at the picnic table where Velma, Jake, and Leopold were waiting anxiously.

'Bug!' cried Velma. (She sounded pleased to see me, which gave me a pretty good feeling.) 'We thought you were dead! Where've you been?'

'Just hanging around,' I said. I introduced Clarissa all round, and wasted a whole minute explaining what had happened.

Leopold looked at Clarissa guiltily – 'I'm sorry I didn't listen,' he said. 'I'm sorry I was a coward.'

'You can be sorry later,' I snapped. 'Right now there's too much to do. The fate of the Garden rests with us.'

'You can't be serious,' said Leopold incredulously.

'There's just five of us! What can we do against thousands?'

'It's true,' conceded Velma. 'The odds *are* stacked against us.'

I took a long look at the group of bugs in front of me – a sugar-addicted housefly, a feisty grass-hopper, and two ants with artistic pretensions. Surely Leopold was right – what chance did we stand? Maybe better just to run for it, head for a new garden while we could? It wasn't even like I'd miss this rotten Garden anyway. But then I remembered little Billy, and I knew I had no choice.

A voice piped up. 'I'm with B-B-Bug,' said Shaky Jake. 'We've g-gotta try at least.' He crawled round and stood by me.

'He's right,' said Clarissa. 'Krag and the wasps'll never let us live.'

Velma shrugged. 'What the heck? Even if I never live to tell it, it'll make a great story. Count me in.' She hopped forwards.

All eyes fell on Leopold. 'It's a suicide mission!' he protested. 'I . . . I don't want to die.'

Who does? I thought. But Clarissa stepped for-ward. Her voice trembled.

'Listen, Leopold. We've just found the freedom to be ourselves, to be individuals. But that doesn't mean freedom to be selfish. Being an individual doesn't mean you can live completely separate from others. You've still got to have friends, and that means you have responsibilities as well. Sometimes you have to forget your own selfish interests and fight for your friends. Even if that means risking your own life . . .'

It was a corny speech, but I knew it was from the heart.

I guess it did the trick too. Leopold cast his head down in shame. 'Oh . . . I'm in too,' he muttered at last. 'But I'm doing nothing dangerous, OK? Nothing.'

'OK,' I said. 'Now – here's what we do. Krag and his troops are going to attack the Ant-Queen at high noon. Most of the ants will be out foraging for food. When they hear the alarm, they'll try to rush back to defend the Queen. That's when the wasps will mount an aerial attack to cut them off and stop them from getting back in the Nest.' I nodded at Velma and Jake. 'That's where you two come in.'

'W-what will we do, Bug?' asked Jake.

Velma knew. 'We've got a little while before mid-day. We'll talk to as many bugs as we can in the Garden. If we can get everyone together – and I mean EVERYONE – we might just be a match for the wasps.' And her smile let me know that, even if she thought our plan stood a snowball's chance in hell, she'd still give it her best shot.

'And what about us?' asked Clarissa.

I looked at her and Leopold.

'That's easy. We'll be down in the Nest,' I said.

17

Of course, getting in was not so easy. I couldn't just stroll down into the Nest and ask to see the Queen. It would take about three seconds before I was stopped by a sentry.

So when we neared the entrance to the Nest, Clarissa and Leopold flipped me over on to my back. I curled my legs up and tried to be as still as I could. Anyone who saw me would think I was dead.

'That's good,' said Clarissa encouragingly. 'You really look dead.'

'Thanks.'

'Just remember,' advised Leopold (who considered himself an expert on all performing arts). 'Think dead!'

The two ants began to drag me along towards the entrance. Clarissa was at the back shoving, Leopold was at the front pulling. Ants can carry many times their own body weight, so they didn't have too much trouble moving me. I did my best to relax and 'think dead'.

After a few minutes we slowed down, then stopped. We were at the entrance.

'Permission to enter,' said Clarissa. Her voice betrayed no emotion, but I could feel her shaking.

I heard a sentry ant's voice from up ahead reply, 'State your report.'

Clarissa's voice was flat and lifeless again. It sounded odd to me this way. 'We encountered this beetle near the pond,' she said. 'We overcame it and are bringing back the body for food.'

'Just the two of you overcame it?' asked the sentry.

'The beetle was old and weak,' answered Clarissa. 'His defences were almost non-existent. We dealt with him easily.'

Steady on, I thought, still playing dead. *Don't lay it on too thick!*

The few seconds the sentry took to think this over seemed to stretch out forever. All the while I expected him to raise the alarm, to call for reserves.

But all he said was: 'Permission granted. Enter the Nest.' And then I was being hauled along again as we plunged once more into the gloomy tunnels of the Nest.

Down and down we went. I kept my eyes shut, but I could hear the steady trudge of footsteps as other ants passed us in the tunnels. At one point we must have hit a deserted stretch, because Clarissa whispered, 'Just how much do you weigh, anyway?'

'Quit complaining,' I answered. 'I'm old and

weak, remember? You had no problems killing me – you should have no problems moving me.'

Meanwhile, Leopold just muttered to himself. We continued our descent.

At last we came to a stop.

'OK,' whispered Clarissa. 'You can get up now. The coast is clear.'

They each grabbed on to one of my wing casings and flipped me over the right way up. It took my eyes a moment to adjust to the gloom. I looked into the sombre faces of my two companions. The white marking on Clarissa's head looked as pale as the moon. I wondered if I would ever see the real thing again in the night-time sky.

'You did a good job getting us so far,' I said. Leopold snorted derisively. He wasn't enjoying himself.

Clarissa just nodded slowly and indicated a tunnel behind me.

'That leads to the royal chamber,' she said. 'It's the cleaners' entrance, so it should be fairly deserted. But be careful.'

'And you two?' I asked.

'We'll round up as many of the individualists as we can,' said Clarissa, reciting the plan for the twentieth time. 'Then we'll go and see the would-be new queen.'

'OK,' I said. 'Let's do it!' I turned to head off down the tunnel that led to the Queen's chamber.

'Wait!' cried Leopold. 'Aren't you forgetting

something?' His voice sounded more peeved than afraid.

My mind raced. It wasn't much of a plan we had, but we'd gone over it again and again. Had I missed something?

'You didn't wish us good luck,' huffed Leopold.

I smiled. 'I reckon we're going to need a lot more than that,' I said. 'But, for what it's worth . . . good luck!'

And with that we went our separate ways, slipping off into the darkened passageways. I charged down my tunnel as fast as I could, driven by a host of fears. *Was I too late? Would Velma and Jake succeed in their struggle against the wasps above the Nest? When this day was done, would the Ant-Queen still be alive? Would* I *still be alive?*

I was so lost in these thoughts that the ant that appeared in front of me took me by surprise.

'Halt,' it snapped. 'What are you d–'

I didn't have time to talk things over. If it was one of Krag's troops, I had to dispose of it. Even if it *wasn't*, I had no time to explain. I slugged it on the head. It fell back – out cold.

'If you're loyal to the Queen,' I said as I passed the unconscious figure, 'sleep well, pal – and let's hope you wake up to a victory breakfast.'

I ran on down the tunnel. And on. I was starting to think that perhaps I'd taken a wrong turning, when I heard noises from up ahead. The tunnel widened, opening out into a great hall beyond.

I crawled up to the mouth of the tunnel, where I poked my head out and looked down into the royal chamber of the Nest.

It was packed full. The Queen was carrying out a daily review of her troops. Every day she inspected a different division of the glorious Ant Army. Today it was Krag's division, so the chamber was packed with his troops.

Krag himself stood to one side. He was pretending to listen politely to the Queen, but I could see he was ready for action. He was almost quivering with excitement.

I noticed with relief that there were several rows of Queen's own personal guards. They would be gravely outnumbered, but at least they would put up a good fight against Krag's forces.

'Most satisfactory,' the Queen was saying. 'That will be all, Commander Krag . . .'

'Not quite,' leered Krag, then he yelled: 'TROOPS! THE TIME HAS COME! FOR THE GLORY OF THE NEST, ATTACK! KILL THE QUEEN!'

His troops let out a blood-curdling roar and charged forward.

I sighed. It had begun . . .

18

Chaos seized the room. Dozens of Krag's troops rushed forwards, savagely clacking their mandibles. They swept onward like a wave of destruction.

I heard the Queen let out a gasp of surprise. Her loyal guards immediately closed ranks around her, arranging themselves into a defensive formation.

There was a terrible din when the two forces met, and the close-combat fighting began. It was a fierce struggle, and the chamber echoed with cries of pain and triumph. The floor was soon littered with the bodies of the fallen as ant battled ant.

I rushed forwards from my hiding place. I picked up the nearest ant – one of Krag's – and hurled it aside. A second ant leapt upon me, biting and stinging and squirting acid. Bad move – it wasn't able to pierce my armour-plated back. I wheeled around and threw it off me, right into two of its comrades.

I could see Krag himself over on the other side of the royal chamber. He was standing on a mound of soil which gave him a good view of the battle-ground. He yelled instructions to his soldiers. I wished he was closer – wringing Krag's little ant neck sounded like a good idea to me right then.

I put my head down and barrelled my way through the throng until I reached the line of guards defending the Queen. They seemed puzzled when they saw me, and were ready to attack, when I heard the Queen's determined voice from behind them. 'He's on our side! Welcome to the war, Mr Muldoon!'

As I fought alongside those guards, I found myself thinking that I had misjudged ants. I'd always thought of them as cold and emotionless, but those royal guards fought with a passion and bravery that staggered me. When one of them fell, another took its place, and they battled tirelessly as wave upon wave of Krag's troops crashed against our line of defence.

But, despite such valour, the tide of the battle began to turn at last. Krag's troops out-numbered us by far. Holes were beginning to appear in our defensive line. It was only a matter of time before they reached the Queen, I thought, as I beat off another attacker. Krag was going to win!

But then it happened – a great shout went up as fresh troops appeared at the entrance to the chamber. 'FOR QUEEN AND NEST!' It was the ants who had been outside. The wasps had failed to prevent them from returning! The loyal ants had made it back to protect their Queen. Velma had done it!

I laughed out loud. 'Velma, I love you! I'll never say anything bad about grasshoppers ever again!'

The new troops fell upon Krag's soldiers, who were now fighting on two fronts. On and on the battle raged. At one point I became aware that Krag had left his vantage point, but I didn't have a chance to consider why – I was busy fighting off two attacking ants.

I have no idea how long the battle took. It seemed like forever. But at last the point came when I realized that most of Krag's troops had surrendered or been killed, or made a run for it. Those who wanted to fight on were being surrounded and subdued. It was over – the attack had failed.

A haughty voice rang out. 'Mr Muldoon!' It was the Queen. 'How nice of you to drop in! In the light of recent developments perhaps now is a good time for you to tell me what progress you have made in your investigation . . .'

I told her everything I knew about Krag's plan.

'Kill me? But a Nest cannot exist without a Queen,' she protested.

'There's your answer,' I said. I pointed to the side-doorway, where Leopold and Clarissa stood with a pack of their individualist ant friends. They led the young Queen behind them.

'Krag was going to put a new queen on the

throne,' I explained, 'but he would have held the real power.'

The old Queen scrutinized her young rival. 'Bring her closer,' she announced.

The guards parted way as Clarissa, Leopold, and the young Queen approached the monarch. The young Queen had a sleepy, distant expression, like she didn't really know what was going on. When they were close, she lifted her eyes drowsily to the old Queen. Suddenly her face crumpled into a look of pure hatred.

'Death to the Queen!' she shrieked. 'Long live the New Queen!' She hurled herself forward at the old ruler, deadly sting at the ready.

Clarissa reached out to grab her, but too late. No guard was close enough. I was too far away. The only person who could do anything was Leopold: Leopold, the ant who had been too afraid even to listen to Clarissa's story; Leopold, the ant who had said, 'The Queen means nothing to me,' and who had refused to do anything dangerous on this mission.

But Leopold did not hesitate. Without thinking of his own safety, he dived forward, pushing himself between the two queens. The young Queen's sting flashed and plunged into Leopold's thorax.

Two élite guards fell upon her in seconds, and they led her away still screaming. But it was too late for Leopold. He lay at the foot of the old Queen whose life he had just saved. She looked down at him mournfully. 'This truly was an ant who put the good of the Nest before himself,' she said.

Leopold lay gasping on the floor. It was clear he was dying. His voice was weak as he recited his final poem.

'If I should die
Down in this Nest,
Think this of me
I did my best
To be myself
And like no other.
And so farewell,
. . .'

He stopped. 'Er, what rhymes with "other"?' he asked.

'Brother?' suggested one of the Queen's guards.

'Mother?' said someone else.

'Yes, yes,' tutted Leopold, 'but they don't make sense for the last line of my dying poem, do they?' His voice was sounding stronger.

I moved closer to him. 'Just how badly injured are you, anyway?' I asked. I couldn't see any wound on him. Maybe the sting had missed?

Leopold looked down at the body he had assumed was broken and dying. He wiggled all six legs experimentally.

'I can walk!' he exclaimed. 'I'm going to live! It's a miracle!'

Leopold looked amazed at what he had done. I

didn't have time to explain it to him. Let him work it out for himself – one of the most important ways of expressing individuality is to risk it for what you know is right.

I grinned. I didn't think Leopold had a selfless bone in his body. Who'd have thought he'd turn out to be a hero? Maybe there was hope for this Garden after all.

I turned towards the Queen and her entourage. 'Where's Krag?' I shouted.

A royal guard stepped forward. 'He ran off with a unit of his élite troops,' he said. 'They went that way.' He pointed in the direction of a tunnel. I charged towards it.

19

I moved through the tunnels with a speed that surprised even me. What kept me going was the thought of Krag. Krag the traitor. Krag the would-be assassin. I couldn't let him get away.

Krag must have known that he was being followed. He decided to turn and fight. I rounded a corner, and came into a small chamber, where Krag was waiting with a squad of six of his élite guards. Krag stood in the foreground.

'So, Muldoon,' he sneered. 'I've been waiting for this moment since we first met. The Plan might be ruined, but it will be a pleasure to take you apart, piece by piece . . .'

He moved forward; his troops followed. I knew I would not stand a chance against them – they would swarm over me in seconds, biting and stinging, and that would be the end of yours truly, Bug Muldoon, private investigator. Still, I would go down fighting.

But then an idea hit me. It wasn't so great, but it

was all I had. I spoke not to Krag, but to the ants behind him.

'Wait!' I shouted. 'Listen to him! Is this really the way of the ant collective? All along Krag has acted for his own good, his own glory. He didn't want to make the Nest stronger by replacing the Queen – he wanted to make *himself* stronger.'

'Don't listen to the ramblings of a mere beetle!' Krag spat. 'Attack! Kill him! Rip him to shreds!'

But the ants had stopped. They looked at each other and shuffled nervously, but made no further move towards me.

'Fools!' shrieked Krag. 'Can't you see? He is my enemy! You must destroy him!'

I pressed home my advantage. 'Did you hear that?' I asked. 'He said "my enemy", not "our enemy". Krag is the worst individualist of them all, and *he* wasn't exposed to any spray. He talks of glory for the Nest, and what he means is glory for *himself*. He's power-crazed!'

The ants kept perfectly still. The tension in the air was so thick you could walk on it. Then slowly, one by one, the soldier ants turned their backs on me and on Krag. The sign was clear – they would do no more fighting that day.

Krag was in a white rage, but he knew that he was no match for me alone. He knew all was lost.

'I'll get you for this, Muldoon, you meddling beetle!' he screamed.

I smiled. 'Big talk for a little ant.'

He looked me straight in the eye. 'I'll be back,' he said. 'The Garden hasn't heard the last of me!' Then he darted off down a tiny side tunnel. I tried to follow, but it was too narrow for me. The last I saw of Krag was his back legs as he scurried off into the darkness towards whatever Fate lay in store for him. I hoped it was a rotten one.

I turned to go back to the royal chamber. A voice stopped me.

'Mr Muldoon?' It was one of the ants who had been guarding Krag.

'The name's Bug,' I answered.

'You were right, Bug,' said the ant. 'Sometimes an ant can't just follow orders. Sometimes he has to think for himself and make a decision.' He glanced at his companions. 'Like we just did.'

'Do I know you?' I asked. Most ants look the same, but this guy seemed familiar. Suddenly I knew.

'My name is Frank,' he smiled. It was the ant who had first led me down into the Nest at the beginning of this whole thing. 'Is there anything I can do to help?'

I nodded. 'Just show me the quickest way up to the surface. I've got unfinished business up there.'

It was a relief to reach the surface once again, and feel the sun on my face. But I was not prepared for what awaited me up top.

Just as the battle had raged below in the depths

of the Nest, so too a terrible battle had been fought above the surface. The grass was strewn with the dead and wounded of either side – on the one hand the wasps, on the other hand an assortment of every other kind of insect to be found in the Garden.

It had clearly been a terrible battle, but the wasps had been beaten. They must have flown back to their nest down at the tree beyond the fence. Now all the other insects were tending their wounded. Some searched for comrades they feared had fallen in the battle. The mood was not one of exhilaration at victory – instead a kind of weariness filled the air. I wasn't surprised – war can have that kind of effect on you.

I picked my way past a gang of horseflies who were already trying to top each other's tales of combat. A familiar voice called out to me. I turned to see Larry, the older brother of Eddie the earwig. I waved hello. I'd pegged Larry for a staid kind of guy – I was glad to see that when the chips were down he had made his stand. When all this was over, I would tell him that his brother Eddie had done him proud. But right now I had other business.

I spotted her up ahead, and the flood of relief I felt surprised me – Velma. She was talking to a ladybird who had broken one wing in the battle. I sauntered up.

'Bug,' she said. 'Nice of you to join the party, but you've missed most of the fun.'

'Don't worry. We had ourselves quite a party

underground as well,' I said. 'Clarissa and Leopold are OK. Jake?'

'He's fine,' answered Velma. 'He rounded up every fly in the neighbourhood – you should've seen it, Bug. We had earwigs fighting alongside cockroaches and ants on the ground, houseflies and bluebottles and bumble-bees flying in battle formation together. It was beautiful! The wasps put up a good fight, but they didn't have a chance.'

'I bet it'll make quite a story,' I said.

Velma and I scanned the Garden. Down at the end of the lawn, the Man from the House was slumped in a deckchair.

'Do you think he had any idea what was going on?' asked Velma.

I shook my head. 'Humans are too stupid to see what's going on around them. He probably just thinks it's a nice summer afternoon.'

'Well, maybe it is now,' said Velma. 'I mean, everything can go back to normal now, can't it? It's over.'

I was tempted to agree. The Garden looked so nice in the afternoon sun: the vibrant green of the lawn, the splashes of colour in the flower bed. You could almost be suckered into thinking it was a nice place. Almost, but not quite.

I knew that it *wasn't* over.

'Not yet,' I said. 'There's one more thing that has to be done, and I have to do it alone . . .'

I glanced ahead to see that he was still there. He was – the Man from the House, sitting in his deckchair in the middle of the lawn. He was still asleep, I made straight for him. There wasn't far to go now, which was good because I was starting to slow down.

I was concentrating so hard on my destination that I didn't see the pock mark in the lawn until it was too late. I tumbled headlong into it, and only just stopped myself from flipping clean over.

I was just telling myself what a close call that had been, when the spider loomed behind me. It had been even quicker than I expected over the grass. It let out a terrible hiss, and visions of doom raced through my mind.

I opened up my rear wings to fly away. It was more a reflex action that a deliberate move. I guess I thought if I could just fly away, I could live to fight another day. But I was too late. The spider pounced and seized one of the extended wings on my back. It tried to yank me back with it. Instead I felt the wing tear clean off my back. It didn't hurt as much as you might expect (although it isn't an experience I would recommend).

I took the opportunity and ran like the wind. There was a dull ache where my wing had been broken off. I told myself to ignore it and keep on running. The spider was hot on my tail.

I was starting to think I would never get there, but then at last I reached my destination – the Man from the House. He was still snoozing, and his legs were crossed so that only one foot was on the ground. I sprang forward and landed on the scuffed toecap of one workboot. I scurried up the front, making sure I didn't catch my legs in the lace-holes. Beneath me the spider clambered on to the boot as well.

I was on the top of the workboot now. I looked upwards, up the Man's trouser leg. His hairy white skin extended up into the darkness. I didn't fancy getting trapped up there.

Instead I jumped out and caught hold of the hem of the Man's trousers. I flipped myself round, then began to run up the front of his trouser leg. At the top of his shin my path was blocked by his other leg, which was crossed over the first. I hopped on to this leg, and climbed up to the top of the knee. Then I stopped and turned. I was done running – this was where I would make my stand.

After several long seconds a hairy leg appeared over the ridge of the knees. The spider came into view. It clacked its fearsome jaws, and moved towards me. Its pace was slow now – almost leisurely – as if it was savouring every moment. I froze with fear.

But I had a plan! When the spider was about to spring, I suddenly bent down and bit at the Man's leg with all my might. This is what I thought would happen: the bite would wake the man up; he would look down to see this big, ugly spider on his leg, whereupon he would see it off with his newspaper. Splat! Meanwhile I would leap to safety.

Nice plan, huh? There was just one small problem: the material of the Man's trousers was too thick. I couldn't bite through to his skin, so he didn't wake up. Two words formed in my mind: BIG and TROUBLE.

The spider edged forward. It knew that I could not fly away with just one wing. It was getting closer and closer. I felt a gentle breeze play upon me from the side.

That was it! I could not fly properly, but I could glide! I charged right towards the on-coming spider. At the last moment I leapt up into the air, extending my single wing and hoping that the breeze would not die. It didn't, and I was lifted over the head of the enraged spider. My one wing meant that I couldn't fly straight, but I'd taken that into account and jumped to one side. I spiralled down on the wind and landed on the Man's other boot.

I wasted no time. The spider would already be rushing down the Man's leg. I scampered up to the top of the boot, up past the crumpled layers of sock, and I took an almighty bite of the Man's bare leg. Then I rolled over and simply fell off. I dropped to the ground like a stone. Whatever happened now, it was out of my control.

The events that followed are blurred in my mind. I heard the Man shout 'YUK!' as he woke up and saw the huge spider on his leg. I saw the spider fall to earth as the Man leapt to his feet. And then I heard the noise as the Man squashed the spider under one of his steel-capped workboots: SPLUDGE!!!!

And let me tell you something – it was the sweetest sound I ever heard.

Epilogue

A few days later I was invited back down to the Ants' Nest. 'Invited' – I liked that a whole lot better than being ordered.

When I reached the royal chamber, I hardly recognized the place. The ants had been busy. You'd never have guessed it had been the site of a bloody battle. The place was packed now. Rank after rank of ants stood in orderly lines. They were waiting for the Queen to speak.

'Order has been restored,' declared the Queen. 'The Nest is One again . . . I decree that Krag's followers will not be punished. They were simply following orders, which is the ant way.'

'Everything back to normal?' I asked.

The Queen was silent for a long while. At last she spoke.

'I am old . . . but I am not too old to learn, and in the last few days I have learned much.' She surveyed the assembled ants. 'The outbreak of individualism did not arise simply from the Man's chemical spray. It came from *within us*. It was Krag's hunger for personal power that nearly brought the nest to ruin. But . . .'

I nodded. 'But what about the Individualists?'

'The so-called Individualists fought alongside my guards with loyalty and courage,' she said. I saw Leopold on the front row puff himself up with pride. The Queen went on: 'But more than that, they have shown us that individualism is not always bad. Indeed, there are times when it is necessary. I have learned that, sometimes, in order to serve the Nest, you have to think for yourself. We are One, but we are a One composed of many parts. For this reason, I have decided to allow the Individualists to continue their . . . activities. Who can say what lies ahead for the Nest . . . but together we will find the right balance.'

The Queen turned her attention to Clarissa. 'As for Clarissa – her work was invaluable, and she will be rewarded accordingly.'

'Hold on,' I said. 'What work?'

Clarissa turned to me. 'I was working for the Queen all along,' she said simply. 'Everything I told you in the spider's web was true. All except one thing – after I overheard Krag talking to the wasps, I *did* come to the Nest and I told the Queen what I had heard. We didn't know how many troops would side with Krag, so we decided to wait and see what would happen. We didn't even know if *you* could be trusted. But before I could find out more, I got caught by the wasps . . .'

I shook my head and laughed.

The Queen smiled politely and said to me, 'Of course, in honour of your services in this matter, Mr Muldoon, you shall be granted the highest honour of all. I shall award you the Order of the Nest. You will become an honorary ant.'

'That's swell, your majesty,' I answered, 'but I'll have to say no. Being a plain old beetle suits me just fine.'

The Queen acknowledged my wishes with a graceful nod.

That's all, I suppose, although of course it didn't just end there. To my mind, no account is complete until you've heard what happened to everybody. So here goes . . .

- Leopold was offered a high-ranking admin. job in the Nest. He turned it down. Last I heard he was trying to set up an improvisational theatre workshop on the patio. I must remember to avoid it.
- Clarissa got a promotion, but she still sings three nights a week at Dixie's Bar. She's a big hit: the joint is standing-room only when she's on.
- And Jake? He's happy as a flea on a sheepdog.

The Queen ordered an entire battalion to spend one month foraging for sugar products, which they dutifully bring to Shaky Jake, housefly and hero.

- Velma was promoted to Chief Reporter in the Garden news service because of her role in cracking the story. She tells me it won't go to her head. Yeah, right.
- After their plan failed, the wasps were on the war-path for a while. I heard the Queen was crazier than ever. But then one of them made the mistake of stinging the grandson who was visiting the Man in the House. Next thing, the Man was seen coming out of the garage with a big can of chemical Wasp Killer. The whole Wasps' Nest had to be evacuated, and the last we heard was that they were looking for a new site several gardens down. Nobody misses them too much.

And what about me?

Well, once all the excitement died down, I was left feeling kinda empty. I knew that peace had been restored, but I couldn't help wondering for how long. How long before some other power-crazed bugs tried to take over the Garden? How long before something else tried to eat me? We lived in a world full of hungry jaws, and I was sick of it. I was sick of the Garden. I was thinking about maybe leaving and heading off somewhere else. Perhaps things *were* better in the meadow?

The thought buzzed around my mind, but there was something I had to stick around for. After a few weeks, it was time.

I asked Velma to take a stroll with me down by the nettle patch. She agreed, but she was puzzled.

'What are we doing here?' she asked. (For a bug, Velma doesn't like the outdoor life too much.)

'Just wait,' I said, and I nodded towards the stem where the pupa was hanging.

It wasn't long before things started. A tiny tremor ran down the hard case of the pupa that Billy the caterpillar had become. I smiled. I had been keeping an eye on it to make sure everything was OK. Now it was time . . .

A hairline crack appeared. It ran the whole length of the case, and it became wider and wider. At last a pair of antennae poked out. A head followed – the head of the butterfly that Billy had become. It blinked at the fierce afternoon sun and heaved the rest of its body slowly out.

At first it didn't look too spectacular sitting there on a leaf. Its wings were small and bedraggled. They hung down limply.

'Is it supposed to look that way?' whispered Velma.

'Sure,' I answered. 'It's got to pump blood through its veins. That'll get the wings up to size.'

And even as I spoke, those wings were getting bigger and bigger right before our eyes.

'It's beautiful,' breathed Velma. She didn't get any arguments from me. This was why I'd stuck around.

The butterfly that Billy had become was breath-taking. Its wings were an explosion of colour – rich blood-red, shot through with velvety black, and dotted with patches of crystal blue. It was stunning. It turned its head in our direction, but it showed a look of total unawareness. That's the way metamorphosis goes – you don't remember anything. It's like being born all over again.

The butterfly held its wings straight out to dry and harden in the warmth. Then, at last, it spread its wings and lifted off into the air.

As I watched it flutter away, I felt a sense of pride. I had helped to keep Billy the caterpillar safe. I was partly responsible for the thing of beauty that Velma and I were watching fly off.

And that's when I realized it. I had to stay in the Garden. I might not have the nicest job going, but the Garden *needed* someone like me. Someone who would do his best to look after the little guys like Billy. It was as simple as that: through these mean flower beds a bug must walk who is not himself mean. I belonged here.

I turned to Velma. 'I'm hungry,' I said. 'Let's go get something to eat . . .'

Let me tell you something about the scarab beetle. They eat horse manure, which they collect and roll up into a ball before consuming. Luckily, I am *not* a scarab beetle.

As we walked away, Velma said, 'Hey, you never did tell me why you're called "Bug"!'

'Velma,' I said, 'it's a long story. Let's go to Dixie's Bar, you and me, and I reckon I'll tell it to you . . .'

The Peppermint Pig

by Nina Bawden

'You can't keep a pig indoors, Mother!'

Mother couldn't see why not. Johnnie was only the runt of the litter, a little peppermint pig. He'd cost Mother a shilling, but somehow his great naughtiness and cleverness kept Poll and Theo cheerful, even though it was one of the most difficult years of their lives.

Winner of the *Guardian* Award

READ MORE IN PUFFIN

An Angel for May

by Melvin Burgess

Tam often takes refuge in the ruins of Thowt It Farm when he is unhappy at home. One day he follows an old beggar woman and her dog to the farm and is transported back to the Second World War. There he makes friends with May, who has been rescued from a bombed-out house and now refuses to eat or sleep indoors. When Tam gets into trouble in the town, May comes to his rescue. She tries to persuade him to stay at Thowt It, but Tam is afraid of being permanently trapped in the past.

Shortlisted for the Carnegie Medal

'An atmospheric, eerie book . . . it handles a time slip in a completely believable way'
– Carnegie Medal judges

The Great Elephant Chase

by Gillian Cross

Penniless and parentless, Tad and Cissie are on the run from the tyranical Mr Jackson. Despite the challenge of rivers, prairies and their assorted inhabitants, Tad is spurred on by Cissie's faith in a proper home waiting for them across America. But hiding an enormous elephant is no easy task, and Tad realizes that he must find courage and determination if they are ever to reach their destination.

'A wonderful tale of children and a performing elephant' – *Daily Express*

'This is writing at its best'
– *School Librarian*

READ MORE IN PUFFIN

Flour Babies

by Anne Fine

Let it be flour babies. Let chaos reign.

When the annual school science fair comes round, Mr Cartwright's class don't get to work on the Soap Factory, the Maggot Farm or the Exploding Custard Tins. To their intense disgust they get the Flour Babies – sweet little six-pound bags of flour that must be cared for at all times.

Young Simon Martin, a committed hooligan, approaches the task with little enthusiasm. But as the days pass, he not only grows fond of his flour baby, he also comes to learn more than he could have imagined about the pressures and strains of becoming a parent.

'Funny and moving, Flour Babies is an uplifting, self-raising story' – *Guardian*

Winner of the Carnegie Medal and the Whitbread Children's Novel Award

John Diamond

by Leon Garfield

Young William Jones discovers that his dying father is a swindler. When he sets out for London to right the wrongs his father has done to his old partner, Diamond, he finds the backstreets less than welcoming and all kinds of horrors lying in wait.

Winner of the Whitbread Award

READ MORE IN PUFFIN

The Wacky World of Wesley Baker

by Gene Kemp

I intend to donate a cup, and I expect you to win it, my boy! . . . We're going to start a whole new programme . . . A WESLEY THE WINNER programme!'

Wesley's life is hard enough as it is. All his family are fitness freaks, while he would prefer to write stories in peace. And Agnes Potter Higgins, the maddest girl in the school, is in love with him and follows him EVERYWHERE! But when Dad decides that Wesley will be the sports day champion and Mrs Warble casts him as St George in the school play (with Agnes as the princess), his world really begins to turn upside down.

'No one writes with more insight into the primary school classroom, its pupils or its teachers than this author' – *The Irish Times*

The Terrible Trins

by Dick King-Smith

'It's big,' said Thomas.
'It's ugly,' said Richard.
'It stinks,' said Henry.
'Is that the one that ate our dad?'

The Terrible Trins are mice with a mission: to revenge the death of their father. Trained to a peak of physical fitness by their mother, the three bold bucks are soon frightening the life out of the Orchard Farm cats – but bad-tempered mouse-hater Farmer Budge has got his eye on them . . .

'Top standard for eight and up'
– *The Times*

'Other writers who put words into animals' mouths are outclassed'
– *The Times Educational Supplement*

The Haunting

by Margaret Mahy

Barney is being haunted. But is he in danger? The insistent ghostly footsteps in his mind move ever closer while his brother and sisters try to unravel the mystery. And as the supernatural events reach a tense climax, the family members learn some surprising things about themselves. Entirely convincing, beautifully written, this quite outstanding novel has become a modern classic.

Winner of the Carnegie Medal.

'Outstanding in the richness of her ideas and her great storytelling ability'
– *Twentieth Century Children's Writers*

A Little Lower than the Angels

by Geraldine McCaughrean

God, the Devil, Heaven and Hell all stand before Gabriel's eyes. He can scarcely believe them. But when he is forced to flee from his cruel master, the stone mason, and leaps into the red, smoking jaws of Hell, he discovers a whole new and exciting life. But will his new life with the travelling mystery players be any more secure than his old one? In a world of illusions people are not always what they seem. Least of all Gabriel.

Winner of the Whitbread Award

Dakota of the White Flats

by Philip Ridley

When Dakota Pink decides to find out the truth about Medusa's baby monster it is the beginning of a quest that will lead Dakota and her best friend Treacle away from the White Flats to Dog Island and the Fortress. Will they manage to escape the mutant killer eels to discover what lies behind the barbed wire of the Fortress and who the mysterious Lassitter Peach is?

Award-winning author Philip Ridley takes his readers on a rollercoaster of an adventure full of thrills and surprises.

'Ridley looks set to be one of the outstanding new writers for older children'
– *Sunday Times*

Timothy of the Cay

by Theodore Taylor

RESCUED: 12-YEAR-OLD BOY PHILLIP ENRIGHT AND HIS CAT FROM UNCHARTED CAY

Phillip has survived, despite being blind, for four months on a tiny, remote, desert island. But although Timothy, the old black sailor who saved him from drowning, died before his rescue, his wisdom and spirit continue to inspire Phillip to risk an operation which might restore his sight and enable him to return to the cay to see it for the first time.

In this compelling story, Phillip's ordeal is dramatically set along side a moving account of Timothy's long struggle to realize his dream of being captain of his own ship.

READ MORE IN PUFFIN

For children of all ages, Puffin represents quality and variety – the very best in publishing today around the world.

For complete information about books available from Puffin – and Penguin – and how to order them, contact us at the appropriate address below. Please note that for copyright reasons the selection of books varies from country to country.

On the worldwide web: www.penguin.co.uk

In the United Kingdom: Please write to *Dept. EP, Penguin Books Ltd, Bath Road, Harmondsworth, West Drayton, Middlesex UB7 ODA*.

In the United States: Please write to *Penguin Putnam inc., P.O. Box 12289, Dept B, Newark, New Jersey 07101-5289* or call 1-800-788-6262

In Canada: Please write to *Penguin Books Canada Ltd, 10 Alcorn Avenue, Suite 300, Toronto, Ontario M4V 3B2*

In Australia: Please write to *Penguin Books Australia Ltd, P.O. Box 257, Ringwood, Victoria 3134*

In New Zealand: Please write to *Penguin Books (NZ) Ltd, Private Bag 102902, North Shore Mail Centre, Auckland 10*

In India: Please write to *Penguin Books India Pvt Ltd, 11 Panscheel Shopping Centre, Panscheel Park, New Delhi 110 017*

In the Netherlands: Please write to *Penguin Books Netherlands bv, Postbus 3507, NL-1001 AH Amsterdam*

In Germany: Please write to *Penguin Books Deutschland GmbH, Metzlerstrasse 26, 60594 Frankfurt am Main*

In Spain: Please write to *Penguin Books S. A., Bravo Murillo 19, 1° B, 28015 Madrid*

In Italy: Please write to *Penguin Italia s.r.l., Via Felice Casati 20, I–20124 Milano*

In France: Please write to *Penguin France S. A., 17 rue Lejeune, F–31000 Toulouse*

In Japan: Please write to *Penguin Books Japan, Ishikiribashi Building, 2–5–4, Suido, Bunkyo-ku, Tokyo 112*

In South Africa: Please write to *Longman Penguin Southern Africa (Pty) Ltd, Private Bag X08, Bertsham 2013*